Claire turned to thank the stranger, but he'd walked away.

The pocket-size Bible sticking out of his back pocket snagged her attention. Interesting.

She hurried after him, not wanting him to disappear without thanking him. In this day and age, not many people would have come to her aid.

"Hey, wait," she called.

He paused, glancing over his shoulder. When she caught up to him, he arched a black brow. His expression was less intimidating now, more playful. She swallowed.

Her first impression that he was good-looking had been marred by the anger hardening his features. She realized he was beyond good-looking and sliding straight toward gorgeous. Everything inside went on alert, like the quills of a porcupine sensing danger.

Books by Terri Reed

Love Inspired

Love Comes Home #258
A Sheltering Love #302

TERRI REED

grew up in a small town nestled in the Sierra Nevada foothills. To entertain herself, she created stories in her head and when she put those stories to paper her teachers in grade school, high school and college encouraged her imagination. Living in Italy as an exchange student whetted her appetite for travel and modeling in New York, Chicago and San Francisco gave her a love for the big city, as well. She has also coached gymnastics and taught in a preschool. She enjoys walks on the beach, hikes in the mountains and exploring cities. From a young age she attended church but it wasn't until her thirties that she really understood the meaning of a faith-filled life. Now living in Portland, Oregon with her college-sweetheart husband, two wonderful children, a rambunctious Australian shepherd and a fat guinea pig, she feels blessed to be able to share her stories and her faith with the world. She loves to hear from readers at P.O. Box 19555, Portland, OR 97280.

A SHELTERING LOVE

TERRI REED

Steeple
Hill®

Published by Steeple Hill Books™

STEEPLE HILL BOOKS

Steeple
Hill®

ISBN 0-373-87312-2

A SHELTERING LOVE

Copyright © 2005 by Terri Reed

This edition published by arrangement with Steeple Hill Books.

www.SteepleHill.com

Printed in U.S.A.

Do to others as you would have them do to you.
—*Luke* 6:31

To Robyn, friends forever. Thank you for all the times you listened. For all the times you were there when I needed you.

Thank you to author and retired social worker Delle Jacobs for so patiently answering all my questions. Any mistakes are purely mine.

Thank you to my editor, Diane Dietz, for believing in me and for the wonderful pep talk.

Chapter One

Here comes trouble.

Maybe some kids were beyond her help.

Claire Wilcox eyed the two teenage boys saunter-ing across the grassy park toward the shaded spot where she and fifteen-year-old Mindy were talking. Claire's gaze zeroed in on the taller, dark-haired boy with scraggly, shoulder-length hair and a thin face. The early April sunlight splintered off the earring dangling in his left ear. In his hands he carried a golden retriever puppy.

Behind the two boys, in sharp contrast, the purity of the majestic snowcapped peak of Mount Hood rose in the distance like a sentry, standing watch over Oregon's Willamette Valley.

She'd seen the dark-haired boy around town.

Some locals blamed last month's vandalism at the downtown theater on this kid. She didn't know his story, but she would soon if the opening of the teen shelter went as planned this coming July.

"Hey, Johnny, catch." The dark-haired boy suddenly tossed the puppy to his blond companion, who awkwardly caught the small dog.

Claire's heart pitched. She stalked forward, her hands clenched at her sides. "Hey! Don't do that!"

Johnny shoved the dog back into the hands of the taller kid.

"Do this?" He tossed the small dog back to his companion.

The puppy yelped and Johnny caught the little fluff ball, then held it at arm's length by the scruff of the neck. The kid's gray sweatshirt and faded jeans were dirty, as if he'd rolled or slept on the ground. His gaze darted away from Claire, his face flushing guiltily.

"Tyler, stop it," Mindy wailed as she moved to the side of the taller kid.

So this was Tyler.

Claire scrutinized the dark-haired boy in his red T-shirt with some rock band's logo on the front and ripped, dirty jeans. Mindy had said he was nice. He didn't look nice. He looked downright nasty. The kind of guy she would have fallen for at Mindy's age. The kind that would give any parent a heart attack.

Not her. She knew better. Everyone deserved a chance.

Claire understood the pain of the rebellious teens she was trying to help. She understood—had experienced the wounds of childhood. Wounds inflicted by those she should have been able to trust.

Teens like Mindy and Tyler stood on the cusp of adulthood, where the choices they made would affect the rest of their lives. By the grace of God, Aunt Denise had stepped in and helped Claire when she'd been at the point of no return. Not every teen was as fortunate.

If only Claire could get through to kids like these. Earning the right to be heard, to be trusted, would take time. Once The Zone officially opened, she hoped to make a difference in their lives. Give them a place to belong, to come to when it became too rough at home.

A safe haven.

But her only concern right now was for the animal.

She flexed her hands and willed herself to stay calm. With as much control as she could muster, she said, "Give me the puppy."

Tyler snorted and grabbed the puppy back from his friend. "You ain't the boss of me, lady."

"No, I'm not. You're the boss of you. But I don't think you're cruel, either, Tyler. Just let the pup go." Though she'd gentled her tone, anxiety wavered in her voice.

Tyler flipped his unwashed hair over his shoulder as his eyes narrowed. Claire met his challenging gaze dead-on. He wanted attention, wanted someone to trust, somebody to care. Well, she'd show him she cared and that she wasn't afraid or intimidated by him.

Most people in Pineridge would just as soon lock up these kinds of teens. The "throwaways." But Claire had different ideas. They needed help and understanding. And she could give that to them.

Tyler dropped his gaze first, affirming to Claire that he just needed some guidance, some boundaries. But when he lifted his gaze back to hers, she sucked in a breath at the malicious intent in his gray eyes.

"You want the dog?" His mouth curled up in a sneer. "Then you catch the dog."

Tyler flung the puppy upward. Fear clamped a steely hand around Claire's heart. The dog yelped again, its legs flailing in the air. She lurched forward, her arms outstretched, her hands ready to catch the dog. But she was too far away. Her feet stumbled on a rut in the grass. Her pulse pounded. The teens' snickering echoed in her ears.

Dear Lord, help!

A shadow crossed her peripheral vision. The air swirled with a rush of heat as a dark shape overtook her, passed her. She skidded to a halt.

A man.

He deftly caught the small pup and cradled the trembling dog against his black leather-clad chest. His big hands gently soothed the puppy with long strokes down its back.

The man was tall, well over six feet, wearing black leather down to his heavy boots. The ebony hair curling at the edge of his collar needed a trim and a few days growth of beard shadowed his square jaw. Tiny brackets edged his mouth and weathered little creases outlined his eyes.

But it was those dark orbs that sent her pulse into shock.

Though he stared down Tyler, she saw the hard

glint of rage shining from the fathomless depths of his black eyes.

Tall, dark and dangerous. Nothing but trouble there.

Claire resisted the urge to back away. She'd learned long ago that she was susceptible to the kind of guy that sent good girls scrambling for cover. Claire wasn't a good girl; she'd done some horrible things in the past. Things she was ashamed of. But she'd turned her life around and wasn't about to backslide.

Tyler scowled. "Hey, mister, that's mine."

"Not anymore." Anger punctuated the stranger's words. His accent wasn't from the Pacific Northwest.

He thrust the butterball of a dog into Claire's arms. His gaze flicked over her before once again settling on Tyler. Claire shivered at the fury in those impenetrable eyes.

She cuddled the puppy close. Its heart hammered against its little ribs. She met Tyler's fierce glare. Animosity glowed bright in his eyes. She wasn't winning any points with the kid. A long, tough road stretched ahead if she wanted to help him. But she was up to the challenge.

"Time for you to leave, little boy," the man said. A command, not a suggestion.

She groaned into the puppy's fur. Not the thing to say to a teenage boy who was trying to grow up too fast. Was the man deliberately trying to provoke Tyler? A quick glance at the tall stranger confirmed what she feared. His expression dared Tyler to react.

Tyler's chin jutted out in a mutinous gesture. "Who's going to make me?"

The man didn't move a muscle, didn't say a word, but the charged silence crackled with suppressed hostility.

He'd have no trouble taking on an undernourished fifteen-year-old, even one with the attitude of Godzilla. Why was the man still so enraged now that the puppy was safe?

Beside her, Mindy shuffled her feet, clearly uncomfortable with the situation. Wide-eyed, Tyler's friend looked between the intimidating man and Tyler. His hunched shoulders and the way he edged away from Tyler told Claire that the blonde would bolt at the first sign of a fight.

The fire in Tyler's eyes slowly turned to fear as the man stood there waiting, his expression intense and unyielding. She held her breath, hoping Tyler would take heed of his own internal warning system and leave.

He didn't.

"I'm not going. Not without the dog." Tyler's voice quivered slightly.

"You might want to rethink that idea."

The steely edge in the man's voice sent a ripple of concern down Claire's spine. Time for damage control. She couldn't let this male posturing go any further. Tyler was just a boy trying to survive in the world.

She stepped toward the stranger and laid a hand on his arm. The leather-clad muscles of his forearm bunched beneath her palm and shot little sparks of heat up her arm to settle in the middle of her chest.

Her hand tightened.

For a tense moment she thought the man wouldn't back down, but then he turned his gaze on her. The burning anger in his eyes slowly drained. Stark, vivid torment filled his expression.

Aching compassion welled within her, making the need to heal, to offer comfort, tangible. She'd seen the haunted expression before, in the faces of teens who'd confronted the unimaginable and survived. But glimpsing the wounded soul of this man made tears sting the back of her eyes.

His eyes widened slightly, giving her the distinct impression that he'd somehow glimpsed her thoughts. Invaded her mind. She blinked rapidly, using her unshed tears as a shield against the threat of this man who twisted her up inside and made her forget to breathe.

Abruptly, he turned away, fixing his attention back on Tyler and giving her a moment to catch her breath. His body language relaxed slightly, giving her the signal that she could remove her hand from his arm. She did, her hand immediately turning cold.

"Go. Just go." The tired, ancient sound of the man's voice gave testament to the pain she'd seen in his eyes. "And don't come back."

Claire opened her mouth to protest, to say she wanted the teens to come, to know that they'd always be accepted at The Zone. But she met Tyler's gaze and the words died in her throat.

Hatred gleamed from his gray eyes. He brought his hand up and made a slicing motion across his throat. The stranger stiffened, all semblance of relaxation vanishing.

Tyler curled his lip and backed up. "Come on, let's blow this dump," he said, his chin jutting out once again.

Relief showed on the other boy's face. "Yeah, this is boring." He didn't waste time retreating, gaining a large lead on Tyler as he headed west toward one end of the park.

Tyler kept backing up, his gaze darting between the man and Claire. "Mindy, let's go."

Claire put a hand on Mindy's slender arm. "You don't have to go. I can help you."

Mindy chewed her lip, her young face pale, scared. Indecision shone in her blue eyes.

"Mindy!" Tyler's demand made the girl jump.

"Don't go," Claire implored.

The puppy squirmed in her grasp and she loosened her hold. Mindy twirled her long, dirty brown hair around a finger, gave Claire an apologetic grimace and scurried after Tyler.

As Tyler's arm settled around Mindy in a gesture that Claire knew all too well, heaviness descended on Claire's shoulders. Billy had possessed her like that. Made her his property. She shuddered and repressed the memory. She was never going to allow herself to be that needy again.

"Lord, please protect Mindy," she murmured the prayer aloud.

Claire snuggled the puppy and turned to thank the stranger, but he'd walked away. His long legs carried him in the opposite direction of the teens, toward the parking lot at the east end of the park. The pocket-size Bible sticking out of his back pocket snagged her attention. Interesting.

She hurried after him, not wanting him to disappear without thanking him. In this day and age, not many people would have come to her aid.

"Hey, wait," she called.

He paused, glancing over his shoulder. When she caught up to him, he arched a black brow. His expression was less intimidating now, more playful. She swallowed.

Her first impression that he was good-looking had been marred by the anger hardening his features. She realized he was beyond good-looking and sliding straight toward gorgeous. Everything inside went on alert, like the quills of a porcupine sensing danger.

He raised both brows. Heat crept into her cheeks. "I wanted to say thank you."

"No big deal."

The soft rumble of his voice vibrated through her, sending tingles along her nerve endings.

He started forward again and she doubled her steps to match his lengthy stride. "But it was a big deal to this little guy…and to me."

One corner of his mouth kicked upward in an appealing way as he scratched the dog behind the ear. "You two take good care of each other."

Claire watched that big, strong hand stroke the yellow fur and envy flooded her. It had been a long time since a man had run his fingers through her hair. A long time since she'd allowed anyone close enough to touch her at all. But this was the wrong man to want that from.

She pushed aside her need for physical contact. "Where are you from?"

"That obvious, huh?"

She grinned. "Most Oregonians don't have an accent."

Both brows rose again. "Sure you do. You just don't hear it."

She pulled her chin in. "Really?"

He laughed and the sound warmed her all over. "Yes, really."

Bemused that she sounded as different to him as he did to her, she probed, "And you're from…?"

"Long Island."

"You're a long way from home."

His ebony eyes took on a faraway glaze. "Yes. A long way from home."

The loneliness in his voice plucked at her. "Where are you staying?"

His gaze came back to her, those dark eyes alight with an unidentifiable emotion. "I'm not."

Curiosity gripped her. "Where are you headed?"

He shrugged again.

A drifter. A twinge of sadness weaved through her curiosity. Did the pain she'd seen earlier drive him to keep moving, to drift through life? Looking at his tall, lean frame, she wondered when he'd eaten last. The familiar urge to help, to do *something*, rose within her.

"Could I make you lunch as a way of saying thanks?" She pointed to the gray two-story building at the north end of the park. "I live there."

He stopped, tilted his head to one side, and studied her. She gave him a smile of encouragement and tried to slow the pounding of her heart. This man with his dark good looks and bad-boy image was just the kind of guy to turn her crank. But she wasn't going to let her crank be turned again only to be left idling on the side of the road. Her smile stiffened.

"Don't you know you shouldn't talk to strangers, let alone invite them in?"

She barely stopped herself from rolling her eyes. She'd heard similar warnings from all the well-meaning people of Pineridge who thought she shouldn't open her heart and home to the teens.

Granted, this man was far from a teenager. But he posed a threat on so many levels that she would be wise to heed the warning. Wisdom was something she was still working on. "I run a shelter. Inviting strangers in is part of what I do."

"A shelter?"

"A teen shelter, to be exact."

"Why?"

She sighed. The infernal question seemed to be at the top of everyone's list of questions and asked in the same wary, derisive tone, though his held more edge to it. "The stigma of runaway teenagers is that they're crazy and out of control. But they're still just kids. Yeah, they're rough and tough and act horribly at times. But deep down most are scared, confused and need help."

"But why *you?*" He seemed genuinely interested.

It was on the tip of her tongue to tell him the unvarnished truth. Why she felt compelled to make him understand was a mystery. So instead she settled for her pat response. "I remember the anxiety and chaos of those teen years. If I can make a difference in someone's life, I know I was put on this earth for a reason."

"That's admirable."

His compliment pleased her, as did the almost wistful look on his handsome face.

"But woefully misguided." His expression hardened. "Thank you for the offer, but I should be heading out."

"Why are you in such a hurry, if you don't know where you're headed?"

He leaned toward her, his jet-black eyes probing and his decidedly masculine scent, full of leather and the outdoors, engulfing her senses. "You're tenacious."

Her spine stiffened and she lifted her chin. "Persistence is a virtue."

Amusement danced in his gaze. "*Patience* is a virtue."

Her cheeks flamed at being corrected. "I consider both to be virtues."

That appealing half-grin flashed again. "Both are admirable traits." His tone dropped to a deep and husky timbre that she found fully alluring. His accent rasped along her skin like a velvet caress. Her knees wobbled and knocked together. "We've established you have persistence, but do you have patience?"

Oh, yeah, she had patience. Hard-won and, at the moment, stretched taut.

Every instinct warned her that this man could endanger her vow to be self-sufficient with nothing more than his smile, let alone how his voice lulled her senses, and threatened to impair her judgment. He could make her want to lose herself in those dark eyes with one glance.

She didn't need or want a man in her life. Never again would she allow herself to be vulnerable to the whims of a guy, to be used and abandoned, forgotten.

She stepped back, needing to put distance between them. She'd offered help. He'd said no. She needed to accept that. Time to stay focused and in control of her own responses.

"Be safe." Her voice sounded breathless. And she didn't like it.

This time there was no half-grin, but a full-blown, toe-curling smile that sent her blood zooming. He saluted and then sauntered to a low slung, shiny chrome-and-black motorcycle with the unmistakable winged insignia of a Harley.

He threw one long, lean leg over the seat, looking at home on the bike. He plucked a black, sleeklooking helmet from where it hung on the handlebars and put it on. A second later the bike came to life with a thundering rumble.

"Hey," she yelled over the noise of the engine and stepped closer.

He gave her a questioning look.

"What's your name?" She didn't know why it was important, but she needed to know.

His eyes widened slightly, then a slow smile touched his lips. "Nick."

His smile made her heart leap. He'd stormed into

her life like a knight of old and performed a heroic deed, all the while putting her female senses into overdrive.

He flipped down the visor on the helmet and rolled away. She watched him turn the corner toward downtown Pineridge and then disappear from sight. It was a good thing he'd roared out of her life before she'd lost her head and done something embarrassing like drool.

"Well." She stood rooted to the ground for a moment as her heart resumed its natural rhythm. She held the puppy up and stared into his sweet little brown eyes. The puppy licked at her face. She laughed and hugged him close. Gwen was going to just love the little guy.

"Well, little Nick, you want to come home with me?"

Nick Andrews couldn't get the pretty blonde out of his head. The woman's heart gleamed in her baby blues and every subtle and not-so-subtle expression that had crossed her face.

Oh, she had courage, he'd give her that. Not many women—let alone men—would have stood up to those punks. She cared for those street urchins. But she might as well have worn a sign that said "Heartache Welcome."

She talked a good game, how they were just kids in need of some help. He didn't believe it.

Thankfully she wasn't his problem. No matter how attractive the package or how much he admired her spunk, he had enough to deal with. He wasn't exposing his heart to the pain of loss again.

He gunned the engine and took the exit out of Pineridge that dropped him onto Interstate 84 headed west toward Portland. As he jockeyed for a position in the traffic, a sharp urge to turn back assaulted him.

He frowned, convinced he was being paranoid.

Yet he couldn't shake the image of Tyler's slicing gesture.

Nah, the kid didn't have the guts to do anything serious. *Just throw a defenseless animal around,* a tiny voice inside reminded.

Nick's jaw tightened.

The kid was a bad seed. Nick had seen eyes like that before. The eyes of a killer.

Man, he'd have pulverized that kid in the park, would have gladly exorcised two years of bottled rage on the punk, if the blonde hadn't restrained him with her gentle touch.

He hadn't even asked her name.

Not my problem.

But yet…

He wove around a slow-moving truck. He shook his head, trying to rid himself of the nagging feeling he should turn back. Serena would have said it was God's nudging, but God had been quiet two years ago when a nudging could have saved her life.

So why would God start communicating with him now?

Twenty miles ahead the freeway split. He could either take the interstate exit for I-5 North heading toward Washington State and on up to Canada or he could take I-5 South toward California.

He was at a fork in the road, literally. Which way

to turn? How far could he go to outrun the past? Where would he find peace? What had he done to deserve such punishment? How could he leave the blonde so unprotected?

"She's not my problem!" he shouted.

The words swirled around inside his helmet until they were sucked out by the rushing wind.

Chapter Two

"Here you go, little Nick." Claire set a plastic bowl full of water on the linoleum floor in the kitchen area. "Nick?"

The puppy had been sniffing around the kitchen floor moments ago. Now the little scamp was out of sight. Claire walked into the open area of The Zone. She looked under the Ping-Pong table that the Jordan family had donated, and behind the brown corduroy sofa she'd found at Goodwill. "Nick, here boy. Where are you?"

She wasn't equipped to care for a puppy. She needed dog food, a collar and a doghouse. Whew, the list was endless and could be expensive. She shrugged. Whatever was needed, she'd find a way to provide. She couldn't turn the dog out any more than she could a human.

"Ah, there you are."

The little fluff ball was snuggled up against a bright yellow beanbag chair. Claire scooped him up and he licked her chin. "Thank you for the kiss. I wonder who you belong to. I'd sure be upset if I'd lost such a cutie." She snuggled her cheek into his soft fur. She'd have to make flyers and post them around town. Surely Nick's owners would be looking for him.

And if no one claimed him?

She would keep him.

She carried him back to the kitchen and set him down in front of the bowl. His black nose sniffed at the plastic rim and then, apparently deciding it was okay, he lapped at the water.

"Thirsty boy." Claire smiled at the ball of fur. Tenderness tightened her chest. She'd never had a dog before. She was excited by the prospect, but her internal monitor quickly warned not to expect to keep him. Somewhere out there were the little guy's owners.

She found a blanket in the closet under the stairs and made a cozy bed on the floor in the kitchen.

"Here you go, Nick," she said, picking up the puppy and setting him on the blanket. He walked in a circle, sniffing at the material.

A bump sounded from beyond the wall of the kitchen. Nick paused; his ears perked up. Claire walked to the window over the sink and peered out. Nothing on the grassy yard stretching to the woods that edged the property. She twisted her head, craning to see left, then right. Nothing.

"Probably a squirrel," she muttered to Nick. "You'll like chasing those when you're older." She wagged a finger at the dog. "I don't think you'll ever catch one, but if you do, don't bring it home. Wherever your home ends up being."

Nick plopped down in the middle of the makeshift dog bed and rested his head on his paws.

"Look at the size of your paws." She shook her head. "You're going to be a big one, aren't you? Just like your namesake."

The image of the tall, dark man sitting on his gleaming motorcycle made her flush again. He was the stuff dreams were made of. A modern-day knight coming to the rescue. But she didn't need to be rescued. She could take care of herself.

What was his story? Where would he end up?

There was something compelling about his dark eyes. She'd seen pain and intelligence, rage and mischief there. The way he'd smiled at her when he'd said his name was enough to make any woman's knees weak. The man was too handsome. But not in a pretty boy way or even a *GQ* way. The angle of his nose, the jut of his whiskered chin and the planes of his cheeks could have been sculpted by a master's hand.

She gave a wry laugh. *Well, he had been, you dolt.* God had done a nice job on Mister Nick. On the outside to be sure, but on the inside…?

A man who stepped in when he saw trouble was a rarity indeed. A man who carried a Bible with him out in the open even rarer. Was he a man after God's own heart?

She'd never know. He was long gone now, just a wonderful memory of a guy on a bike who'd offered his help and wanted nothing in return. Definitely a rarity.

A man like Nick would be hard to resist. Good thing she wouldn't face that temptation again.

With a quick glance to make sure the puppy still slept, Claire headed for her office—a small room located in the front of the house. It was an ideal spot to work and still be able to keep an eye on the main area of The Zone.

The bedrooms were all upstairs and she'd taken the largest of the five bedrooms at the far end of the hall. Gwen's room was at the top of the stairs while the other three rooms were in various degrees of readiness for taking on more teens. Not that Gwen was a teen any longer. She was a college student now with a part-time job—a far cry from the strung-out, skinny orphan Claire and Aunt Denise had first brought home.

Having Gwen come into their lives solidified Claire's desire to start a shelter. She'd decided to open it here in Pineridge because no such facility existed in the area.

But there would be soon.

Claire sat at her desk and rummaged through files and notes. There was still so much to do before she could officially open. More government hoops to jump through, the community to convince and teens to build trust with.

And a puppy to care for. She compiled a list of needs for Nick. Just in case she was unsuccessful in finding his owners, she wanted to be prepared. Then she went to work on her plans for The Zone.

The clock ticked by another hour.

The hairs on the back of her neck raised and chills raced down her spine. Something wasn't right.

The loud shrill of three fire alarms pierced the quiet. Heart pounding with dread, she jumped from the chair and raced into the living room. A gray haze hung in the air, stinging her eyes and burning her lungs.

Fire!

"Nick!"

She raced toward the kitchen. Smoke billowed from beneath the crack in the back door and through the open window over the sink, filling the room with frightening quickness. She heard the puppy whimper, but she couldn't tell from where.

She dropped to her knees like she'd been told to do in elementary school. She crawled across the floor toward the kitchen. The heavy smoke swirled around, making it difficult to see.

The puppy's blanket was empty. She crawled out of the kitchen. "Nick!" she called again, taking in smoke. She winced as her lungs spasmed. In the laundry room she found the puppy huddled in a corner, its little body shaking.

"Here, boy." Claire scooped the pup up and cuddled him close.

Claire crawled toward the front of the house while holding Nick in one hand. She breathed in. Coughed. Her lungs burned. She caught her hand on the leg of a chair and went down on her elbow, her knees scraping on the floor. Nick yelped as she tried to catch herself with the hand that held him.

The smoke became dense, more intense. The front door seemed a mile away. Somewhere in the closet under the stairs was a fire extinguisher. She'd get Nick out, come back for the extinguisher and put out the fire.

She crawled forward again, laboring to breathe. Tears streamed down her cheeks. The puppy whimpered.

"It'll be okay, Nick. Dear Lord, please let us be okay."

She coughed, her breaths coming in short, shallow gasps. Her stomach rolled. She paused, waiting for the dizziness to pass. It didn't. She forced herself to continue on despite the effects of the smoke. Her survival instinct pushed her, urged her to keep crawling away from the source of the smoke.

Her wrist gave out, forcing her weight down hard on her elbow, sending pain up her arm. Her head fell forward to smack against the hardwood floor. Spots of light popped in front of her eyes.

She couldn't stop, she had to keep going.

Where was the man in black leather when she needed him?

Flames shot from the back of the house.

Nick's heart slammed against his ribs as he stopped his bike at the bottom of the cement stairs leading to the front door. He set the kickstand and jumped off his bike. He rushed up the porch steps and burst through the front door.

Smoke billowed around him, stinging his eyes. His gaze zeroed in on Blondie crawling toward the door with the puppy clutched to her chest with one hand, while she balanced with the other hand.

She lifted her head, her eyes wide. The puppy

squirmed out of her grasp and ran past Nick's legs and down the steps.

Nick scooped up Blondie and carried her to the front yard where he gently laid her down on the grass. She opened her mouth to say something but coughed instead. He rolled her to her side as she spit out black soot between taking in gulps of air.

Relief surged through Nick. He'd finally given in to the urgent, nagging feeling that he should turn back. And a good thing, too. He patted her shoulder, offering her comfort as his heartbeat began to slow.

"You came back," she said in a hoarse whisper.

"Yeah," he acknowledged.

"The puppy?" she rasped, her eyes widening as she sat up and was momentarily gripped with another bout of coughing.

"He ran out. I'm sure he's fine."

She raised her gaze to her home. "My building."

The disappointment and hurt in her voice burned in his gut. This shouldn't have happened. He knew who was to blame. His fingers curled into a fist. He'd make sure they paid.

Seeing that the blonde was out of danger, he rose. He refused to consider why he felt the need to help her, why her distress tightened a knot in his chest. "I'll see what I can do."

He left her on the grass and went around to the back of the building where the smoke seemed to originate. Two garbage cans were on fire directly below an open window as well as the wooden slats of the back porch.

Pillows of black smoke rolled into the kitchen.

The flames were licking at the back door and the ceiling of the porch, curling the gray paint and blackening the wood, which crackled and snapped.

Nick skirted around the fire to where a garden hose lay rolled on the ground. The faucet turned easily and water sprayed out. He aimed the spray on the door and porch since that would be where the damage would be most devastating.

Off in the distance the wail of a siren drew close, bringing hope of help. Within minutes firemen bustled about, waving off Nick and his efforts. He dropped the hose and headed back toward where he'd left Blondie.

He spotted her as he came around the corner and his chest tightened more. Grass clung to her hair, streaks of soot marred her creamy complexion and smeared her white blouse and jeans.

Two paramedics were tending to her. Or rather, trying to. She brushed away their attempts to get her into the ambulance. Nick stepped over a fire hose as he approached.

"No, I can't leave," she said as she dodged one EMT and snagged the arm of a passing fireman. "Do you know how much damage has been done?" Her voice rasped with the effects of the smoke. A purple goose egg formed on her forehead.

"Not yet, ma'am."

She dropped her hand away and the fireman continued on, giving Nick a nod as they passed each other.

The worried lines framing her mouth deepened and her eyes were troubled as she turned to face Nick. She closed the distance between them in a rush of steps. "Is everything ruined?"

The anxiety in her voice tore at his heart. He didn't want to care. He couldn't. "Hard to tell. The fire department will let you know. You need to go with the paramedics and let them check you out." He took her elbow and steered her back toward the ambulance.

"I need to find the puppy!" She doubled over, coughing.

He held fast as she tried to pull away from his hold on her elbow. "What you need to do is let them take care of you."

"But who's going to take care of things here?" She made a sweeping gesture with her hand. "I have to be here."

"Is there someone, a friend, a family member, you could call who could come?"

Two little lines appeared between her dark blond brows. "This place is *my* responsibility."

Was she a control freak or did she really not have anyone she trusted to help? What did it matter to him, anyway?

But it did matter. This happened because of *him*. His interference. He felt responsible for her. For her situation.

"I'll tell you what. I'll stay—make sure the police and the firemen have everything they need—while you go with the paramedics."

"You'll stay?" Big tears filled her eyes. She rapidly blinked them away.

That knot twisted another notch, warning him he was getting too involved. But guilt was a stronger motivator than self-preservation. He owed her a debt because he'd brought this on her.

He gave her a reassuring smile. "I'll stay."

She sagged and allowed him to help her into the ambulance.

"Wait," she called as he stepped back. "You'll find the puppy?"

"Sure."

Her smile held gratitude. "Thanks. His name's Nick."

Their gazes held for a moment before the doors of the vehicle closed.

Nick stared after the ambulance. She'd named the puppy after him. Flattered warmth spread through him, heating his face. He was treading water in the deep end.

Not my problem?

He scoffed. "Yeah, right."

Claire sat on the gurney waiting for the emergency-room doctor to return. She swung her bare feet, picked at the cotton hospital gown and tried to ignore the noises from the other exam rooms.

She felt vulnerable and exposed, but mostly she was worried. Worried that everything she'd worked so hard for was ruined.

She chewed her lip, wondering if Big Nick had found Little Nick.

The corner of her mouth lifted at the memory of his expression when she'd told him the pup's name. He'd looked dumbfounded.

She still could hardly believe God had answered her prayers by bringing Nick back. When he'd come storming into The Zone she'd thought she was dreaming. Dreaming about a dark warrior who used his powers for good, not evil. Like some comic book character, except the strong arms that had held her so tenderly had been very real.

And the concern in his eyes called to her in a way nothing else could. It had been a long time since anyone had shown any real concern for her well-being. Oh, people had shown her kindness, but she often felt it came from obligation to her late aunt's memory rather than for herself.

The need to belong to someone rose sharply and she squashed it like an irritating fly. She couldn't allow herself to want anyone, to expect anything from anyone because expectations only led to disappointment.

More likely, Nick wouldn't stick around as he'd promised. She sternly steeled herself against any pain from hope. She wouldn't fret over it, wouldn't let it matter.

She was thankful he'd arrived when he had and that she hadn't inhaled too much of the smoke. The doctor had said her lungs might hurt for a few days and she'd probably have a headache from smacking her head on the floor, but otherwise she was in good health and could return home. He'd gone off to tell the nurse to discharge her.

But what would she be going home to?

Her stomach twisted. She had a pretty good idea who'd set the fire, but she hadn't told the police when they'd arrived because she wasn't a hundred percent certain.

She had to focus on moving forward no matter

how much this incident set her back. She'd push through it, as always.

First she had to get back to The Zone. She didn't have money for a cab with her. She shrugged. She'd walk. She didn't relish putting on the smoke-scented clothes she'd arrived in, but she'd do what she had to.

The nurse pushed aside the curtain and stepped in. She was tall, African-American and very striking. Her black hair was pulled back into a fancy twist and her smile was kind.

In one hand she held a clipboard and in the other a brown paper bag, which she set on the counter. "The doctor says you can be released. I have a few forms for you to sign." She handed Claire the clipboard and pen.

Quickly looking over the form, Claire worried her bottom lip. She wasn't sure how the bill would be paid—if the insurance would cover it or not. She signed where appropriate and handed the clipboard back. She'd deal with the financial stuff later. "Where are my clothes?"

The nurse moved to the counter behind the gurney and picked up a clear plastic bag that contained Claire's dirty clothes. Wrinkling her nose, she said, "You're not going to want these anymore."

She set the bag down again and then grabbed the brown paper bag she'd brought in and handed it to Claire. "Your boyfriend brought you these. When you're dressed, come on out."

Claire blinked. Boyfriend? She opened the bag and pulled out her red polo shirt and fresh jeans. Embarrassed heat crept up her neck and settled in her cheeks.

Someone had gone through her things.

Nick?

A jittery panic hit her stomach like a spray of pebbles. He couldn't be her boyfriend. Not in a million years. She didn't need a boyfriend.

But she had to admit it felt good to have someone care.

Anticipation quickened her pulse. She put on the clothes. Finger-combed her matted mop of hair. Then sedately walked out from behind the curtain toward the administration desk.

Her nervous flutters fled, replaced with a melting warmth as Nick unfolded his long, lean frame from a chair and strode to her, reminding her of a dangerous panther stalking its prey.

And to her utter dismay, she realized she wanted to be hunted.

"The doc said you're okay," Nick stated by way of greeting as Blondie—Claire, he corrected himself—slowly drew nearer to him.

He'd waited to come until after the fire engines had disappeared and the investigators had finished scouring the area for clues to the arsonist. He'd answered the investigator's questions and told them what he could about Blondie and the teens.

She'd changed into the clothing he'd brought her. Smudges of soot stood out in stark contrast on her pale face. Her hair poked out in different directions with bits of green grass peeking out here and there. He stifled a smile.

She was adorable, vulnerable and in need of protection.

In need of help from someone other than him.

He'd get her settled safely, then leave.

She blinked up at him. "What are you doing here?"

"Came to get you. I didn't figure you'd have a way back. I hope the clothes are okay. Your roommate, Gwen, picked them out. She was pretty upset but I told her you'd call her as soon as you could. She had to get to work or she'd be here now."

"Thanks. I'm glad Gwen did the responsible thing and didn't come here." She tucked a strand of hair behind her ear. "How…how bad is the damage to the building?"

Anger flared in his gut at what those punks had done. "The porch is gone. You'll need a new back door."

They headed toward the doors of the hospital. "And the puppy?"

He slanted her a glance. "*Nick* is fine. I found him in the park chasing bees."

Ducking her head, she chuckled. "I hope you don't mind that I named him after you. I didn't think I'd see you again."

He held the door open. "I'm flattered."

To his amusement, her cheeks turned pink. "I guess I'll have to call him Little Nick. So I don't get you two confused." They walked in silence for a moment before Claire glanced back up at him. "Thanks," she said.

"For what?"

She stopped and tilted up her heart-shaped face. "I could have died if you hadn't rescued me."

The glint of admiration in her baby blues spread through him, making him think of knights, damsels in distress and fire-breathing dragons. Making him feel like a hero.

Stupid.

He was nobody's hero.

"You were almost to the door," he said.

"Why did you come back?"

"You wouldn't believe me if I told you." He ushered her to the parking lot where he'd parked her little green four-wheel drive Subaru.

"Try me." Her eyes widened. "Uh, thanks for bringing my car."

He lifted a shoulder as he unlocked the door and held it open for her. "Gwen gave me the keys—we didn't think you'd want to ride on the back of the Harley."

A gleam of longing entered her blue eyes. "Actually, I would have liked that."

He raised a brow. "Then I'll take you for a spin before I leave."

The hunger in her eyes set his blood to racing at full throttle on an open road, then abruptly she shook her head and wariness entered her gaze. "No, no. That wouldn't be such a good idea."

She climbed in the car and primly folded her hands in her lap.

Nick shut the door, grateful for the reprieve. The thought of her with him on his bike with her arms wrapped around his waist sent a shiver through him.

Not a good sign.

He wouldn't allow himself to become attracted, attached or anything else to her.

Gotta keep moving, he warned himself.

Chapter Three

Driving with Claire down Pineridge's main street, Nick surveyed the town with a jaundiced eye. Small-town America. He'd passed through so many over the last two years, they tended to blend together.

Redbrick storefronts with large, single pane windows lined both sides of the wide cement sidewalks. Every few stores sported a blue awning over the doorway. Nick barely glanced at the pedestrians moving at a sedate pace from shop to shop, going about their lives. He didn't want to consider an old man's frown or a young mother's smile. Didn't want to make a connection with anyone.

On both sides of the main street, about ten feet apart, stood a lone birch tree with a small square patch of dirt at its base. Kind of like himself, part of the whole, but separate.

On the west side of the main drag, cars parked between white angled lines. Red bricks indicated the crosswalks instead of painted lines. The street signs were tall, white posts with arrow-shaped slats and street names printed in bold black letters. The white posts rose out of large, round, colorful flowerpots. At each intersection, old-fashioned black metal lamp-posts added charm to an already charming community.

A family sort of town. A place to raise kids, watch summer parades and grow old in. A place he couldn't easily disappear into. A place where he didn't belong.

All the buildings were the same height. No high-power skyscrapers here. The perfect place for a woman like Claire, he thought, glancing over at her. Generous and kind. Open and friendly. A big city would eat her alive.

At the far end of town, he turned down the side street that led around the park.

The Zone came into view, a solitary structure flanked by empty lots. A lone police car sat at the curb in front. Nick parked behind the police car. Claire was out and up the cement front stairs before he had opened his door.

As he followed her inside, the puppy barked a greeting and raced to Claire. She bent and scooped him up for a quick hug. "Oh, you sweet little thing. I was so worried about you."

Nick's gaze focused on the officer rising from the couch. This guy had been here earlier. His uniform was starched and his badge shined. Not a single strand of hair was out of place. His young, clean-shaven face led Nick to guess the man to be in his early twenties.

The officer gave him an assessing once-over before focusing on Claire. "Good to see you're okay, Claire."

Nick didn't like the way the man said her name with such familiarity. And he didn't like that he didn't like it.

At least she didn't go all moonie-eyed. Not that he cared.

She set the animal back down. "Thanks, Bob. What are you doing here?" Without waiting for his reply, she walked toward the kitchen where most of the damage had been done by water. "Did the fire department say anything? How it started?"

Granting Nick a suspicious glance, Officer Bob walked to where she stood. "The fire started in the garbage cans. Whoever did this probably didn't expect the building to catch on fire. But it was sloppy work."

Nick stepped over to the counter and perched on a stool. "It was the teenagers from the park."

Claire's glare took him by surprise. "We don't know that for sure."

Officer Bob narrowed his gaze. "Which teenager?"

"Like I told the others, I came across two boys harassing Claire this afternoon in the park," Nick said to the officer, but his gaze was riveted on Claire. He couldn't figure out why she'd protect them.

Claire's gaze was direct and pleading. "I didn't see who did it."

Officer Bob cleared his throat. "Maybe *he* did it."

Nick's gut clenched. The unfounded accusation rankled worse than a bottomed out stock market.

What a lame, backwater-cop thing to say. Nick stared at the officer. Bob glared at him with more than just suspicion. Jealousy filled his hazel eyes. So that's how it was, Nick thought. Officer Bob had a thing for Claire.

"That's ridiculous, Bob. He saved my life."

"Maybe he set the fire to stage saving you."

Claire gave Nick a can-you-believe-this look and then rolled her eyes. "Tell him you didn't do it."

"I didn't do it," Nick stated flatly.

"See, there you go. He didn't do it." Claire put the puppy down and then heedlessly splashed through the thin layer of water on the kitchen floor to the sink.

Bob folded his arms across his chest. The stance only emphasized his thinness. "He's not from here, Claire. What do you know about him, anyway? He could be a serial arsonist, for all you know."

Nick snorted, gaining himself another glare from Bob.

She filled a bowl with water, her movements efficient and unhurried, then carried the bowl to the living room where she set it on the dry floor for the puppy.

She straightened and leveled a stern look on Bob. "I know he's from Long Island, that he's traveling through town, he carries a Bible in his pocket, he stopped to help me when he didn't have to and his name is Nick. That's all I need to know."

Nick blinked, touched that she'd so soundly defend him without really knowing anything more than she did. That she noted his Bible pricked his curiosity about her faith. She was too trusting and way too giving.

She needed a protector.

He wasn't about to apply for the job, but he had a feeling that old Bob would sure like to.

"I want to see some ID," Bob snarled at him.

Irritated to be the subject of the officer's suspicion, but grateful someone was watching out for Claire's interest, Nick dug his wallet out from the inside of his leather jacket and handed Bob his driver's license. "Did they find anything useful?"

"That's privileged information." Bob shot him a dark look. "I'm going to run this through the computer." He turned to Claire. "I'll be right out front if you need me."

She gave him a bland smile.

As soon as Officer Bob was out the door, Nick asked, "Why didn't you want him to know about the kids? You could have been killed."

Images flashed in his mind. The cloth shroud covering Serena's body. The blood stains on the sidewalk. The headstone at her grave site. His insides twisted with unspent rage.

"We don't know that they did it," she defended.

"And we don't know that they *didn't*. Come on, Claire. You know that kid's likely to do something."

"You heard Bob. *Whoever* did it was trying to scare me with some smoke. They weren't really trying to burn the place down."

"You could have passed out and suffocated if I hadn't come back!"

"*Might* have. And you did come back."

He shook his head. "You gonna wait until they seriously harm you before you make them take responsibility for their actions?"

"You don't know that they did it," she repeated, clearly exasperated and defensive.

"Then let the police prove they didn't do it."

"No! I'm not going to accuse someone without proof. If the authorities find clues that implicate them, then so be it. But I won't help them along."

"Instead you're going to wait for those punks to pull something else? Something worse?" Something like what had happened to Serena. He shuddered.

"I can take care of myself."

He scoffed. "Give me a break. Lady, you're a disaster waiting to happen." A disaster he wanted to avoid.

"Excuse me? I don't think you have any right to say that."

She was right. Nick stared at her. When had he lost his mind?

When he'd come within an inch of throttling a punk over a puppy and started this whole mess. He should be halfway to somewhere else by now, not here arguing with Blondie.

But the woman was intent on putting herself at risk. Responsibility weighed heavily on his shoulders, dragging him under.

What he wouldn't give for a life preserver right about now.

Pulsing with annoyance, Claire planted her hands on her hips and glared at Nick. "I have done perfectly well before you rolled into my life, thank you very much."

He spread his hands wide in a gesture of entreaty. "Hey, just stating the obvious. I've known you less than twelve hours and I've saved your bacon twice. Facts speak for themselves."

"My life is not a disaster."

"Ho!" Nick held up a hand, palm facing out. "I didn't say your life's a disaster. I don't know anything about your life. I'm just saying people will take advantage of you if you're not careful."

His words hit her like a slap upside the head. She'd been taken advantage of before. Billy had taken advantage. Used her. Squeezed her dry and then abandoned her without a second's hesitation.

But she was to blame for allowing him into her life, her heart. For needing him.

Well, she knew better now. She didn't need anyone. Certainly not a tall hunk with a blinding smile who threatened her resolve without even trying.

She had to send him on his way. Now. "Look, I appreciate your help. I thank God you were here, but feel free to go. I'm going to be fine."

"You won't be safe until the police find out who did this. What if next time Gwen's here? You willing to put her life in jeopardy, too?"

She frowned, hating the tremor of fear sliding along her limbs. As long as Gwen was under her roof, she was responsible to keep her safe, as well. "You're right. I'll mention to Bob that maybe Tyler might know something about the fire."

He gave her an odd look. "You and Bob an item?"

She pulled in her chin. "No. Not even. We've known each other since high school. His family lived next door to my aunt Denise. He's not my type, anyway."

One corner of his mouth kicked up. Her pulse did a little two-step.

"What is your type?" he asked.

Mysterious, gorgeous, a heartbreaker. Like you. The thought sent ribbons of heat winding through her bloodstream, warming her face. "I don't have a type," she stated firmly and spun away.

She walked to the back door where charred wood and curled paint spoke volumes. It could have been so much worse. A wave of helplessness hit her, threatening to overwhelm her. This was going to set her back both financially and time-wise.

She squared her shoulders. Somehow she'd manage. She always did with God's help. She didn't—wouldn't—need anyone else.

"It's really not as bad as it looks," Nick said.

She turned to see him rising from the stool. He shrugged out of his leather jacket, revealing a black T-shirt stretched taut over wide shoulders and well-defined muscles. His boots squished through the grimy water on the kitchen linoleum as he approached.

His tanned face bore traces of the sooty smoke that burned in her lungs. That explained why she was breathless. From inhaling too much smoke.

He stopped next to her, his attention on the wall. "Mop up the water. Replace a few boards. Sand and paint. It'll look good as new."

She sighed. If only it were that easy. "Did I thank you for saving me?"

Amusement gleamed in his eyes. "You did."

"Good. You should leave now."

He widened his stance. "You trying to get rid of me?"

She blinked. "Yeah, I am." She had to for her own sake. "This isn't your problem and I'm not your responsibility," she said, her tone harsh.

A flash of something—hurt, maybe?—made his eyes seem impossibly darker. "That's what you really want?"

It wasn't. She felt safe with him around. Liked having him around. Which was exactly why he had to go.

"Yes, it's what I want."

He didn't say anything. Just stood there, tense and hard. His face became a mask of granite, the angles and planes unyielding. "And if I refuse?"

She swallowed and winced at the painful reminder of what had happened. She didn't have the strength to physically make him leave and she didn't know if she could find the strength again to ask him to leave. Not when all she really wanted was to have him hold her. To feel those strong arms around her. To have him tell her everything would be okay. To save her again if she needed it.

Weak.

"I can only hope you'll be a gentleman."

His mouth twisted into a harsh smile.

The front door to The Zone opened and Bob walked back in. He scowled as his gaze jumped from her to Nick and back. "You okay?"

Thankful for the distraction from this confrontation with Nick, she turned and smiled. "Yes, Bob," she said patiently.

She knew Bob was trying to be helpful—to show his concern for her—but it felt more like he was trying to control her.

"Mr. Andrews." He handed Nick's license back to him. "When are you moving on?"

Nick leaned against the counter. "When I'm sure Claire's safe."

Bob's scowl deepened. "I'll make sure she's safe."

"Excuse me." Claire waved her hands to get their attention. "I'm right here, remember, and I don't need either one of you to keep me safe."

"Until we apprehend who did this, you sure do." Bob gestured toward the burned wall. "We don't know they won't come back."

"On that we agree," Nick chimed, giving her a pointed look.

She blew out a sharp breath. She'd promised. "You might talk with a boy named Tyler. He could know something."

Bob pinned her with an intent stare. "I'll see what I can find out."

A knock drew Claire's attention. She left the two men and their meddling to open the front door. Surprised, she smiled at the brunette standing on the other side. "Hi, Lori. What—"

"I heard what happened. Are you okay? Rumor has it a handsome man rescued you." Lori Pearson, who she knew from church, peered over Claire's shoulder. "Is he in there? With Bob?" Lori's smile brightened considerably. "You poor thing. Two men."

Claire laughed with wry amusement. "It's good to see you. Please, come in." She stepped back so Lori could enter.

Lori paused. "You sure you're okay?" Genuine concern shimmered in her dark green eyes.

Flustered, Claire smiled. "Yes. I'm fine."

She didn't know Lori well enough to confide in her. To tell her that she was all jumbled up inside from her feelings about Nick and the fire.

She and Lori had met at a church gathering over a year ago. Lori seemed to find everything amusing. Claire enjoyed Lori's outgoing personality and positive view on life. Though at times Claire felt crowded by Lori.

Claire started to shut the door behind Lori when she heard her name. Peggy and Steve Jordan, followed by their three kids, thirteen-year-old Nathan, twelve-year-old Lisa and the youngest, at six, Matthew, hurried up the walkway.

Peggy came up the stairs looking fresh in rust-colored denims and a colorful peasant-style top with bell sleeves. Her waist-length chestnut hair was held back with a clip. She pulled Claire into a quick hug.

"I couldn't believe it when I heard what happened." She held Claire at arm's length, inspecting her. "You're not burned or anything?"

The display of affection pleased her. Claire stepped back. "No, I'm good."

Steve patted her shoulder. "If you need anything

at all, you let us know." He was a big man with large muscles and a kind smile.

"Thank you." Claire moved aside so they could enter.

Nathan, as tall as his mother, ducked past her without a word. Lisa gave her a shy smile, and Matthew stared at her for a moment with his round green eyes and sweet expression. "You have grass in your hair," he declared before following his family.

Claire reached up and ran her fingers through her hair, mortified to imagine how she must look. She shut the door and took two steps when there was another knock. She quickly opened the door to find her aunt's best friend, Sandy Wellington and her husband, Dave.

"Hello, Sandy, Dave."

Sandy grasped her hand. Her short dark, graying hair curled becomingly to frame her round face. "Dear, we came to see that you're all right."

Dave stepped over the threshold. His silver hair was swept away from his forehead and he wore dark slacks and a blue oxford button-down shirt. "Sandy was beside herself when we heard the news."

"I'm okay. Really." She could see the doubt in Sandy's blue eyes. Claire smiled reassuringly. "Please, come in."

The Wellingtons were kind and thoughtful people. They had also been instrumental in helping Claire on the way to realizing her dream of The Zone.

She took a quick peek outside to make sure there weren't any other visitors before shutting the door.

The women and children had congregated at the edge of the kitchen, while the men had ignored the water to inspect the damage. Peggy Jordan shooed her children away, instructing them to go busy themselves. The oldest two went to the Ping-Pong table while Matthew sat in a beanbag chair to play with the puppy.

Claire's gaze landed on Nick. He leaned casually against the counter that separated the living room from the kitchen. Lori stood close by, smiling up at him. Something unfamiliar twisted in Claire's chest.

She started forward, trying to discern what she felt. The corner of Nick's mouth lifted at something Lori said. Claire's steps faltered. She realized with sickening clarity that she was jealous.

Nick only half-listened to the animated brunette in the pink blouse. His attention kept straying to Claire. Every time someone new entered, she acted as if she were unaccustomed to people caring about her, worrying over her. Why in the world wouldn't they? It was obvious these people were fond of her.

The Jordan family was friendly and he'd appreciated the way Steve had assessed him and then greeted him with a firm handshake. Mr. Wellington was honest in his wariness, had asked point-blank what his intentions were toward Claire, as if he were her father or favorite uncle.

He respected the man's forthrightness and had answered truthfully that he was passing through and had no designs on Claire—only that he wanted to make sure she was safe before he headed out again. His honesty had earned him a quick nod of approval and a pleased smile from Mrs. Wellington before they moved on to look at the damage with Officer Bob, who acted the tour guide.

The brunette—Lori, was it?—said something mildly amusing and he gave an obligatory smile. She put her hand on his arm, her fingers cool and inviting. He shifted out of her reach but smiled again to soften the rejection to her obvious interest. She was Claire's friend, after all. "How long have you known Claire?"

Lori sighed, clearly getting his hint. "For a while now." Her gaze turned speculative. "She's a hard person to get to know. Lots of walls up."

Nick raised a brow. He didn't see walls. He saw lots of open doors that invited trouble. He saw a woman protecting a puppy, protecting kids. "She seems pretty outgoing to me."

"Oh, don't get me wrong. She's definitely not the shy and retiring type. She's very sweet and giving, it's…" She pursued her lips in thought. "She doesn't talk much about herself. More concerned about others. Which is something I don't encounter often in my line of work."

"And what line of work would that be."

"I'm a hairdresser. Cheaper than a psychologist and you get nice hair."

He smirked and glanced at Claire. She looked tired, but her smile came quickly as she talked with the children before moving to where the adults had gathered in the kitchen. Mrs. Wellington had found a mop and was sopping up the waterlogged floor. Claire frowned before she bustled in and herded everyone into the living room. Then she traipsed right back into the kitchen, grabbed some sodas out of the refrigerator and began handing them out.

Not only did she need a protector, she needed a keeper. Someone to carry part of the burden she insisted on taking. He rolled his suddenly tense shoulders.

No way should that person be him.

Chapter Four

"Claire, dear. Stop fussing. We should be the ones serving you." Sandy took the soda cans from Claire's hands and put them on the counter.

"Thank you." Claire allowed Sandy to steer her away from the kitchen.

"You need rest. There's nothing that can't wait until tomorrow."

"But I really need to make some calls. Find out how soon someone can come to fix this mess," Claire protested.

Lori stepped up to flank her on the other side. "I can make your calls for you."

"That's sweet of you, Lori. But no." Claire's gaze darted between the two well-meaning women. "Really, you two. I can take care of things myself. I prefer it this way."

Lori shook her head, her brown hair swishing softly. "See. I told you," she addressed Nick. "Walls."

Claire's cheeks flamed. They'd been talking about her?

A soft, affable smile played at the corners of his mouth. His gaze traveled over her face, searched her eyes. She could feel the magnetism that made him so self-assured, so compelling. She blinked and quickly looked away before she succumbed to the pull he had on her.

"Lori, be nice," Sandy admonished gently, then she turned back to Claire. "What can we do to help you?"

Claire shook her head. "I don't know. Nothing at the moment, but if I think of something, I'll let you know."

Sandy frowned. "You really don't have to do everything on your own."

But she did. She couldn't rely on anyone. Wouldn't allow herself to. As long as she didn't have expectations of others, she wouldn't be disappointed.

Of course, she couldn't voice that thought, she didn't want to hurt their feelings. So instead she smiled politely and changed the subject. "How are Allie and Garrett? Will they be coming to visit soon?" Allie and Garrett were the Wellington's fraternal twins. They'd gone off to college last fall.

Sandy patted her arm with a knowing sigh. "Yes, they will be here this summer. I have an idea. Why don't you come home with us? You could stay in Allie's old room."

Claire dropped her chin. "Oh, no. I couldn't impose."

"It wouldn't be an imposition at all," Dave said as he stepped to his wife's side.

"Or you could come to our house," offered Peggy, as she and Steve joined the circle around Claire.

"That's sweet, but really…" she trailed off as panic flared. Things were spinning out of her control. Everyone meant well but she didn't want to need them. Didn't want to have to rely on anyone for anything.

Bob came around the group and stood beside Nick. The two men were so different.

Bob was good-looking, with his light brown hair and wiry build, in a very boy-next-door kind of way that appealed to some women. Not her, though. He was nice enough and they got along okay. He'd asked her out on several occasions over the years, but friendship was as far as their relationship could go. He just didn't do it for her.

She preferred Nick's near-black hair, dark eyes and towering muscular frame. His cool and dangerous demeanor appealed to her, making her pulse race and her brain sound alarms. He was the kind of man she didn't need in her life.

"You can't stay here alone." Bob pinned her with his hazel eyes.

Claire ground her back teeth at his high-handed tone. "I'm not alone. Gwen lives here, too."

Sandy piped up. "She can come to my house, too."

"Or she can stay with me," Lori offered.

Everyone started talking at once. Only Nick remained silent, his black eyes watchful. Her gaze slid away from him as she tried to reason with the people who were intent on arranging her life. She hated when people tried to arrange her life.

"Excuse me, everyone," Nick's voice, though low, rose above the chatter, effectively cutting off the noise. "Claire's been through a rough ordeal today. I'm sure she could use some time and space."

Surprised by his understanding, Claire's eyes widened.

"Of course." Peggy took her hand. "You let us know what we can do to help."

"I will. I promise." Claire's heart squeezed slightly at the woman's offer of help and friendship.

"Okay, kids, let's head out," Steve said as he took the puppy from Matthew and set him on the living room floor. He led his family out of The Zone.

Before they headed to the door, Sandy and Dave elicited a promise from Claire to call if she needed anything. Nick walked out with them.

Claire watched his retreating back with a frown and fought the ridiculous urge to cry. She'd asked him to leave, but she'd thought he'd at least say goodbye. There she went again—expecting something, only to feel hurt and rejected.

Would she ever learn?

Lori leaned in close, her gaze on Nick as well, and whispered, "He's certainly a prize worth holding on to."

Claire shook her head, feeling suddenly very tired. "You're too much the romantic," she whispered back.

Lori's eyes twinkled with mirth. "Bob, will you walk me to the shop?"

He looked surprised. "Why?"

"Because I asked you to, you big lug." Lori rolled

her eyes. "Men." Then to Claire she said, "I'll check on you tomorrow."

She held up a hand as Claire opened her mouth to protest. "I know, but I'm coming, anyway." She wrinkled her straight nose. "It smells ghastly in here."

"I'll light some scented candles," Claire said.

"You shouldn't stay here," Bob said, his expression hard, concerned.

She tried for patience. "You sound like a broken record. This is my home. I'm not leaving. Besides, the damage is mainly outside. The water's only on the first floor and contained in the kitchen. I'll be fine."

"You are so stubborn." Exasperation echoed in his voice.

"Okay, time for us to go," Lori declared, linking her arm through Bob's. She gave Claire a meaningful look. "I'll talk with you later."

Too weary to argue, Claire nodded. "Fine."

Lori led a reluctant Bob out, leaving Claire alone.

Her lungs hurt and her throat felt like sandpaper. The place did smell and it looked horrible—all black and charred on the back wall around the door. But it was *her* place. The only thing she possessed worth anything. And someone had tried to wreck it. She blew out an angry breath. She wasn't about to let anyone destroy her dream.

A wet tickle at her ankle reminded her she now had one other possession. She bent and scratched behind Little Nick's ears. "Hope you don't mind that it's just you and me, little guy."

She straightened and moved toward the stairs when the front door opened and Nick walked back in.

A surge of happiness tore through her, catching her off guard. She trampled down the giddy pleasure. "I thought you left."

"Sorry to disappoint you." His expression was unreadable but there was a tension in his body she hadn't noticed before.

"No. No disappointment. I'm glad to see you. I mean…I wanted to say goodbye."

"I came to get my jacket." He strode past her to where his leather jacket lay on the stool by the counter.

"Oh." A bubble of disappointment popped in her chest. He hadn't come to see her or to say goodbye.

He slipped the jacket on and crossed the room to stand a few feet from her. "I hear you might have a room to rent."

"You know of a teen in trouble?"

He gave her a sharp look. "I'd intended to stay awhile wherever I stopped this evening. My bike needs a tune-up. And now that it's getting late, I might as well stay in Pineridge. Steve recommended a mechanic a few blocks away."

Her heart pounded in her ears. He wanted to stay here? "That's not a good idea."

One side of his mouth curled up into a lopsided grin. "You'd be doing me a favor. And I could pay you by doing the work to repair the back of the building. That way you don't have to put any money out on expensive contractors and I can have a roof over my head. It would sure beat sleeping on the ground."

"There are hotels downtown. And a Motel 6 on the outskirts, just as you come off the freeway."

He shook his head. "I'll take my bedroll to the park."

"You can't do that. You'll get arrested."

"Your front grass will do."

"No. That's ridiculous."

Claire worried her lip, conflicted. On one hand she didn't like the idea of anyone invading her space. And he would definitely be an invader. But wasn't that the point of The Zone, to rent the rooms so kids wouldn't have to sleep on the ground? That was why Gwen lived with her, because she had nowhere else to go.

Nick wasn't a teen, but he obviously needed a place to stay for awhile. And apparently couldn't afford a hotel. She couldn't turn him out. She could only imagine the cost to his pride to have to ask for help. She knew her own pride held her back from asking anybody for assistance.

Yet, she couldn't shake a strong suspicion that somehow this was all just a ruse concocted to keep her under his protection. Why did he suddenly need his bike tuned up? You're being paranoid, she told herself.

Nick interrupted her thoughts. "I won't get in your way."

Heat crept up her neck. She was taking an awful long time to answer his question. Stalling, she asked, "You could fix the wall and the porch?"

"Yes. I've done carpentry work in the past."

Having him take care of the repairs would save her time and money. He was offering to work in exchange for room and board.

He needed a place to stay. She had it to give. Even though it wasn't a fair exchange. He would work harder than the rent she could charge. "I have a room. But I insist you let me pay you a small wage for the work."

He frowned. "Not necessary."

"It is to me." She wouldn't be a charity case. She'd use the money in the building fund for his wage, and insurance, she hoped, would pay for the repairs.

He considered her for a moment. "Okay. Deal."

He held out his hand. She slipped her smaller one into his. Warmth spread up her arm and wrapped around her senses. Looking in to his dark, commanding eyes, she felt the force of his attraction drawing her in. She sent up a silent prayer for strength to resist such a glaring temptation.

She was determined not to end up paying with her heart.

The strain of the day settled in Nick's neck as he lugged his saddlebag into The Zone. He'd taken his bike to the mechanic, a nice guy with an obvious love of Harleys. Nick had walked back to find Claire nowhere in sight and the front door unlocked.

Somehow he was going to have to get it through Claire's pretty head that safety was important. The quicker she learned that, the quicker he could leave.

He was relieved she'd agreed to let him stay, but

the offer of a wage was too much. And so was Claire. Paying him to do the work appeased her stubborn sense of independence.

He would return the money she paid him with a little extra thrown in to help her cause when the time came for him to leave.

And he would leave. In the past two years he'd found that moving on was the only way to keep from going nuts.

But not until those punks were found and punished. Not until Claire was safe. He couldn't live with any more guilt.

Little Nick gave him a wet welcoming kiss when he'd opened the door, and now chewed at his shoes. He rubbed the pup behind the ears. "I'm counting on you to grow up to be a good guard dog."

Little Nick wagged his tail in response.

A noise on the stairs drew his attention. Claire, dressed in a light blue pullover T-shirt tucked into navy shorts, her blond hair pulled back into a ponytail, stood poised on the top stair. Her face was scrubbed clean of the soot from the fire and her blue eyes sparkled, reminding him of the Caribbean Sea on a clear day. Warm, inviting. A place you don't want to leave. He would make sure to keep their relationship on a purely superficial level. He couldn't afford to allow Claire to add another wound to his already battered soul.

He straightened as she came down the stairs.

"That didn't take you long."

"Caught the mechanic just as he was closing up. He seems to know what he's doing."

She flashed him a quick smile. "Do you want to freshen up?"

"Sure." He felt grimy and could use a shave. His jaw was beginning to itch.

"This way," Claire said over her shoulder as she headed back up the stairs.

He followed, his gaze appreciative of her feminine curves, her long athletic legs, trim ankles and dainty toenails painted a pale pink. She led him down the hallway past one closed door that she said belonged to Gwen and past two rooms that he could see would eventually be bedrooms, but at the moment were in disarray with boxes and mattresses propped against the walls.

She stopped at the fourth room. Stepping in, she flipped on the light.

From overhead, a soft glow illuminated the room, showing a twin-size bed made up with crisp white sheets and a dark green quilt folded at the foot of the bed. A mirror hung over a six-drawer dresser and a bedside table sported a brass lamp, the only other furniture.

She tugged on her lip with her teeth. "I hope you'll be comfortable. I only have twin beds in the rooms."

He quirked his mouth. He'd slept on a twin at his parents' house as a boy. His high-rise apartment on Lexington had had an oversize king. The apartment he'd shared with Serena. An ache throbbed in his chest. "I'll manage."

Claire ducked past him, moved to another open door and flipped on the light to reveal a bathroom decorated in pale blues and creams. "The shower gets fairly hot. Clean towels are in the cupboard under the sink. You can pile your dirty laundry by the door. I'll start a load before I go to bed."

"Great. Just like a hotel." Only here the proprietress was a leggy blonde with caretaking issues. The last thing he needed in his life.

Humor shifted in her gaze. "Bed-and-breakfast."

"Boarding house."

She grinned. "Teen shelter. Thus the twin beds. I hadn't planned on a full grown man sleeping here."

Nick's shoulders tensed. "You okay with me being here?"

"Yes, of course." Her cheeks reddened.

"If you're uncomfortable, I'll head to the nearest Motel 6."

She put her hand on his arm. Her warm touch soothed the tension gripping his insides.

"Really. I'm glad you're staying."

He searched her gaze, not sure what he expected to find. Certainly not the trust shining in her crystalline eyes. "You've done a nice job making this place homey."

Her smile was quick, grateful. "Thank you. I still have a ways to go. Especially now with the fire…" Her smile faltered momentarily, then she shrugged. "But now that I'm paying you to help, it will all come together."

"Are you always so optimistic?"

Her smile dimmed. "I try. It makes life easier to think positively rather than dwell on the negative. I'm not in control of the future or the past. The only thing I can control is my reactions, my choices."

"Right." He'd never been a success at letting go of the past. Even before Serena's death. Nor was he good at not trying to manage the future. Serena had called him obsessive. He was simply the way God made him.

"I can do all things through Christ, who strengthens me,'" she quoted softly.

"So, you are a believer?" That answered his question about her faith.

"Yes. And you are, too, right?"

His mouth twisted at her question. "I believe, but my faith isn't so strong these days."

That was an understatement. He didn't understand God. Didn't understand why He let bad things happen to good people. He definitely didn't understand why Serena had to die. Nick imagined he felt a lot like how Job must have felt.

Claire's eyes were troubled and concern radiated from her in waves. "Maybe coming to church with me on Sunday would help."

He liked her thoughtfulness. "Maybe. I don't know."

"The offer always stands. In fact, you don't have to come to my church. There are other churches in town. God doesn't care what building we worship in as long as we worship."

"I'll take that under consideration." Not liking the direction the conversation was headed, he changed the subject. "Tell me something. How do you expect homeless kids to pay rent?"

Her laugh was soft, husky, thrilling. "I don't. This isn't a business for profit. I plan to offer the teens who are serious about getting their life together a place to stay. Along with the room, comes responsibility."

"What kind of responsibility?" he asked.

"Helping out here, as well as working toward reconciliation with their parents. And if that isn't possible, then getting a GED and making a plan for the future. Finding a job. Going to school. Becoming a useful part of society. Most people just need someone to believe in them before they can believe in themselves."

"Impressive, but faulty. What about the ones that don't want to get their lives together? The ones that would rather steal, cheat and lie than earn an honest way in life?"

Two little lines creased between her brows. "Deep down, no one truly wants to live like that. And if someone doesn't offer these kids a way off the street, their souls wither and die. They feel that no one cares. So why shouldn't they lie, steal and cheat?"

He admired her earnestness. "One lone woman can't save all the homeless kids in the world."

Her chin went up. "No, of course not. But I can make a difference here in Pineridge. Be a safe haven for those that need it. Get to kids before they run to a place where they become just one more body lost in the crowd."

"Is that how you and Gwen hooked up? Was she a teen in trouble?"

She lowered her voice. "Yes. Gwen was living on the streets in Portland. Strung out on drugs and starving. But she's come a long way. All these kids need is someone to care. I will be their someone."

Respect for her tenacity and determination wound through him. She was a force to be reckoned with. He reached up and tucked a stray lock of hair behind her ear. "Lucky kids."

Her breath hitched and her eyes widened. She stepped back. "Uh, are you hungry?"

"Yes, I'm hungry." He liked the way her lips were full and a soft rose color. She had lips made for kissing. He wanted to kiss her, to somehow partake of her idealism, her faith. *Foolish fantasy.*

"Pizza okay?"

He forced his gaze up to meet hers, his brain suddenly sluggish. "Pizza?"

"I was thinking of ordering a pizza to be delivered since the kitchen's pretty much out of commission."

"Right. Pizza would be good." *And a cold shower.*

"What would you like?"

A long sweet kiss. "Pepperoni, cheese, whatever."

"Great." She stepped back and bumped into the wall. "I'll go call." She turned and fled, the door closing with a slight click behind her.

Nick dropped his head to the doorjamb. He had to get a grip. He shouldn't be thinking about kissing Claire. That would only lead to disaster. He would *not* allow himself to become attracted to her.

The sooner he got the work done and those kids caught the better. Then he could go.

Forget about The Zone being a safe haven. It wasn't for him. Not with Claire around.

Oh, my.

Claire leaned against the door. Her heart thumped

in her chest, the rhythm as erratic as her thoughts. Her reaction to Nick was bad. Very bad.

But everything inside her wanted to throw open the door and invite Nick in.

She hadn't been this attracted to a man since… well, since Billy. And she and Billy had only been seventeen. Nick was a full-grown man with the entire powerful draw that went with maturity.

It wasn't that she didn't find men attractive. Bob was good-looking, but he certainly never evoked this kind of response in her. There'd been a guy named Sean in college. Handsome, with a bit of an edge that had satisfied that wild streak in her, and a counselor at Young Life to boot. He'd seemed perfect. Aunt Denise had even approved, but Claire just couldn't let him in. The risk was too great, caring too dangerous.

There were other men in town. Single, available men who'd made it clear they wanted to date her. But she didn't want to date. Didn't want to ever be vulnerable to the whims of the male species again.

So why did she wish Nick had kissed her? It had to have been her imagination when she'd seen his eyes flare with interest, his head dip slightly, bringing his strong jaw and firm mouth closer.

She hurried to the side of the bed and knelt. She needed to spend some time with God, praising Him for his protection and asking Him for strength.

Because temptation would be sleeping just down the hall.

Chapter Five

The evening sun painted the sky with vibrant oranges and pinks. Claire loved this time of day when the world was winding down, becoming peaceful. If she listened carefully she could hear the first few crickets singing their nighttime serenade.

She sat on the front steps of The Zone with Nick, the doors and windows wide open because the acrid smell of smoke still permeated the air. But on the faint evening breeze, Claire did detect the soothing scents of the vanilla, bayberry and lavender air fresheners she'd placed around the inside of The Zone.

Little Nick frolicked in the grass and around the bushes, his body a flash of color against the greenery. Tenderness filled her chest. If Little Nick's owners claimed him, she would get another puppy.

Claire watched Nick devour his slice of pizza. He ate like a starved man. She offered him the other piece sitting untouched on her plate. "I'm not going to eat this. Do you want it?"

He slanted her a sharp glance. "You eat it. One measly slice isn't enough to keep you going."

Her natural reaction was to bristle at his censure and not eat, out of rebellion. She didn't like being told what to do. But the concern in his licorice-colored eyes belied her frustration. He wasn't trying to control her.

She picked up the slice of pepperoni pizza and bit into it. Okay, she was still a bit hungry. The approval in Nick's expression sent shivers along her limbs, making her want to preen under his warm regard. Pathetic. She concentrated on eating.

"So you never told me what made you come back," she said once she finished.

Nick wiped his hands on a napkin, his expression turning pensive, uncomfortable. "I had a strange feeling that I was supposed to."

Claire's spirit quickened. She kept her smile to herself. God had been watching out for her this day. "I'm glad you listened."

He gave her a sidelong glance before closing the lid on the pizza box. "There's enough left over for lunch tomorrow."

"Uh-huh," she murmured. His big strong hands captivated her attention. The sun had kissed them a golden brown. His nails were neatly trimmed. Her gaze traveled up his muscular forearms, past his biceps to his broad shoulders. She shouldn't be so attracted to him. He wasn't wearing black and leather now.

When he'd come down after his shower, her breath had caught in her throat. He'd walked down the stairs looking like he'd just walked out of the pages of a magazine. Khaki pants, with little creases indicating where they'd been folded, and a white polo style shirt stretched taut across his chest. And he'd shaved.

His strong jawbone was now smooth. His dark hair was damp and combed back from his forehead, the ends curling gently at the collar of his shirt. Would his hair be soft and silky or coarse and thick? She itched to run her fingers through his hair.

She usually didn't go for the preppy look. But there was still an edge to Nick. Something wildly attractive that spoke to her, to the restless girl inside. She wanted to snuggle close and share his warmth.

Where was that puppy!

"What are you thinking?" Nick asked.

The heat of embarrassment flushed over her. "I was wondering about you. Wondering why you're here. Where's your family?"

His jaw tightened. Something dark slithered into his expression. She remembered his rage earlier. Remembered the haunted expression that had clawed at her.

My faith isn't so strong these days.

Something had happened to him, something bad. She ached inside. She wanted to help.

Abruptly, he stood and stretched out his hand. The glow from the porch light reflected off the hard angles of his face. "It's late. We both could use some rest."

She blinked, took his hand and allowed him to pull her to her feet, his grip strong and sure. She craned her neck to look up into his face. "I'm sorry if I offended you."

His expression softened. "You didn't offend. You have every right to wonder about me."

"But you're not going to tell me."

A slow smile touched his mouth. "Not tonight."

All right. His words were a promise. He'd tell her when he was ready. She could live with that. She had to earn trust before others would open up to her. She'd learned that in Young Life training. Ha! Who was she kidding? She'd *lived* it.

"Tomorrow you'll need to contact the insurance company. They'll want to come out and assess the damage. If you want, I could deal with them," Nick said.

"I can take care of it," she responded quickly.

He nodded. "I'll be here if you need me."

This was her responsibility. Speaking of which, she realized the puppy had disappeared. "Here, Little Nick, here, boy," she called.

The yard in front of The Zone wasn't big. Two green patches of grass edged both sides of a cement walkway, one Japanese maple tree, a lilac bush and a couple of unidentified bushes. She wasn't much of a gardener. "Here, boy," she called again.

Nick whistled between his teeth, one strong blast. A bush rustled, then a yellow ball of fur burst out.

Claire laughed. "That was good. I'll have to learn that."

Nick scooped up his namesake and handed him to her. "Do you have food for him?"

She gasped. "No. In all the chaos today I forgot to go to the store."

"Where's the closest one?"

"Through the park and left three blocks."

"I'll be back soon."

"Oh…" She wanted to say he didn't have to go for her, that she'd manage. But this wasn't about her. The dog needed food. She should be grateful. She *would* be grateful. "Thank you. I…we appreciate it."

He flashed her a grin, warming her as if the sun shone bright on her skin. She longed to bask in the glow, but knew if she did, she'd only end up with a bad sunburn for her folly.

"Be back soon. Lock the door." With those parting words, he strode away. She stood on the porch holding the puppy and watching him fade into the darkness.

She put the puppy inside the laundry room, closed the door, then picked up the leftover pizza and jumped in her car.

A half hour later, Claire slipped back inside The Zone. Thankfully, she'd made it back before Nick. There was no doubt in her mind that he'd have been standing at the door, arms crossed over that broad chest and his eyes sparking with anger, if he'd returned to find her gone. Relief pounded in her chest. She didn't relish explaining her errand because he wouldn't understand.

She noticed Gwen's coat hanging on the coatrack by the door. Better warn her about their unexpected houseguest. Claire went up the stairs and knocked on Gwen's door.

"Come in."

Claire eased open the door and as always was struck by the color in the room. Gwen had painted one wall a deep burgundy. The other walls were covered with anatomy charts. Gwen wanted to become a doctor.

Gwen was colorful herself, with her long, bright red hair pulled to one side and plaited into a thick braid. She wore powder-blue velour sweats. Her amber-colored eyes smiled at Claire as her freckled face split into a grin.

Gwen bounded from her spot in the middle of her bed, causing several textbooks to crash off the sides, and launched herself into Claire's arms, hugging her and checking her for injuries. "You're okay? I called the hospital from work and they said you'd been released. But you weren't here when I came home. I thought…well, it doesn't matter what I thought because you're here."

Claire laughed and extracted herself from the nineteen-year-old's enthusiastic embrace. "I'm fine. Really."

Gwen nodded once sharply. "Good."

She went back to the bed, picked up her books and arranged them around her as she sat cross-legged in the middle and focused her attention back on her studies.

Typical Gwen. A burst of emotion and then back to business.

In the beginning when Claire and Aunt Denise

had brought Gwen to live with them, the outbursts were wild, loud and dramatic. But keeping a job and going to school had forced the girl to learn to show her emotions in more appropriate ways.

Claire was proud of the young woman's growth. "Gwen."

Gwen lifted her head. "Yes?"

"We're going to have a guest for awhile."

She raised an auburn brow. "Oh?"

"Nick. You met him earlier, right after the fire."

"Ohhh," Gwen said, in a knowing way that grated on Claire. "Mr. Charming in black."

"He needs a place to stay and he's offered to repair the fire damage."

"Right."

Claire ignored Gwen's smirk. "Anyway. Just make sure you're not strutting around in hot rollers and your icky green mask."

Gwen laughed. "I will."

With that settled, Claire headed back downstairs and sat on the couch with Little Nick resting beside her. She closed her eyes and though her voice sounded raspy and her throat hurt a little, she sang softly.

A few minutes later a soft knock sounded at the door. Little Nick jumped to his feet and barked.

"Shhh, now, it's only Nick," Claire admonished as she went to open the door.

Nick gave her an irritated look. "You should always ask who it is before opening the door."

She drew back. "I was expecting you."

There was a disapproving set to his mouth as he moved past her. "You need to be more careful."

Claire didn't like the way her heart hammered in her chest or the panicky way her stomach contracted. She didn't need his approval. She shouldn't be feeling guilty. She didn't owe him anything. She didn't need him.

He fed Little Nick from the small bag of puppy food he'd carried in. "You okay?"

He stepped closer, oblivious to her inner turmoil. His masculine scent washed over her, making her aware of his size and appeal.

"Tired." *And too close to you.*

"It's been a long day."

She fidgeted. What was she supposed to do now? How were they supposed to proceed? She'd better figure it out quick if he was going to be staying there.

She paced away from him. They were adults; they had a business arrangement. There wasn't anything personal about it. She drew herself up. "Well, good night then."

"Good night, Claire." His smile was soft as he headed up the stairs, leaving her to deal with her grown-up loneliness.

And yearnings.

The day after the fire, Claire was awakened by voices. Through the foggy remnants of sleep, the voices sounded a long way off. But as she sat up and memory flooded in, she knew they were coming from inside The Zone. She glanced at the clock. Eleven in the morning. She never slept that late. And amazingly, she couldn't remember waking during the night. She must have been more exhausted than she'd realized.

She grabbed a long pink cotton robe and threw it on over her blue cotton pj's. Barefooted, she padded down the hall, past Nick's closed door to the top of the stairs. She paused to listen.

The unmistakable rumble of Nick's voice slid over her like fingers strumming a guitar. Each chord hummed through her. She struggled to quiet those accordant notes.

Other male voices joined in, though she couldn't make out their words. Cautiously, she padded down the stairs and peeked over the railing. At the large square coffee table, Nick and three men—Steve Jordan, Dave Wellington, and a man she didn't recognize—looked at some papers strewn across the flat surface.

"Nick?"

His smile of welcome sent tingles sliding over her skin. She pulled the robe tighter around her as if she could ward off the effect he had on her.

He stood up and moved to the foot of the stairs. "Sorry to wake you."

"That's okay. What's going on?"

"Volunteers to help," he said with a gesture toward the men staring at her.

She waved, before backing up a step to where she couldn't be seen. "Volunteers?"

He came up a few steps and shrugged. "I went to the hardware store earlier and they showed up wanting to help."

"But I'm paying *you* to do this." She didn't want anyone's charity. Or pity.

His expression hardened. "It will get done quicker with more bodies."

She searched his face, hoping to see something, anything that could reassure her that trusting him was a good thing. All she found was determination. "Fine."

"It'll be okay, Claire. I promise."

She lifted her chin. "Promises can be broken."

"Not by me, they aren't." He turned and walked away, his wide shoulders stiff.

Claire sank to the stairs. She wanted to trust that such a thing could be true. That he was a man who didn't break promises. Besides Aunt Denise, she didn't know anyone who didn't break a promise. And obviously, someone had broken a promise to Nick.

Her heart beat in her throat. Everything inside her wanted to heal him. Only she didn't know how. She had to get him to open up to her, trust her. *Lord, give me the wisdom, the words to say.*

She ran upstairs to get dressed. She had a man's mind to pick.

In her room, she threw on her old faded blue jeans and a purple top. She twisted her hair up and secured it with a clip. Grabbed her old Keds and some socks. When she came back downstairs, Nick and the other men were in the back. She rescued Little Nick from the laundry room and headed outside.

As she turned the corner, Nick saw her and smiled in greeting. She hugged the puppy close to her chest and watched as Nick excused himself from the other men. She put the puppy on the ground. He promptly scampered away.

"Have you called the insurance company?" Nick asked.

She started. "No. I'll go do that right now."

One side of his mouth quirked up. "Good idea."

She ran inside, found her insurance information and made the call. Her agent was understanding and said they'd send someone out right away.

When she went back out, Nick was alone, sitting on the porch with the puppy curled up at his side.

"Where'd everyone go?" she asked.

Nick tilted his head up to look at her. "Until we have the okay from the insurance company, we can't do much."

She sat down beside him. "The insurance adjuster should be here this afternoon."

"Great."

This was her chance to pick his brain, to get him to open up. "How long will your bike be in the shop?"

"A few days."

She ran her hand over the puppy's smooth coat. "How long have you been traveling?"

He glanced at her. "A couple of years."

"That's a long time. What made you decide to ride across the country?"

Her question sliced through Nick. He blocked out the grief welling up. He couldn't go there right now. He didn't know if he ever could.

He stood. "Hey, how about we run to a store where we can get some things for this little guy? I've heard that crate training is the way to go."

Claire blinked up at him, her clear blues showing

disappointment. "Okay." She rose. "I also need to stop at the copy store and run off some flyers about him. I'm sure whoever owns this little guy is looking for him. Let me grab my purse." She disappeared inside with the puppy trailing behind.

A dull throbbing started behind his eyes. "Oh, Lord when will You ever grant me peace?"

He certainly wouldn't find peace with Claire wanting to know about his past. The only way he could handle the pain was by not dealing with it. If he wasn't careful, her stubbornness and determination would wear him down. He couldn't allow her in. Wouldn't allow himself to care about her.

"There you go, boy," Claire said as she put Little Nick inside his new crate. They'd decided to place the crate under a window in the living room where the puppy would get some fresh air.

The pet-store clerk had advised allowing the puppy to get used to his new bed by putting him in and leaving the door open so he could go in and out. The crate should become his refuge.

But for how long? One day, Little Nick's true owner would claim him.

She pushed aside the pang that thought caused.

Where was Nick? After setting up the puppy's crate, Nick had gone outside and not come back in.

Just as she was putting another load in the wash, she heard her name being called.

"Hello, I'm back here," she yelled loudly over the sound of water filling the washer.

Lori walked in wearing faded cut-offs, a yellow,

flowered shirt and beat-up tennis shoes. Long tendrils of dark hair escaped from her ponytail. In one hand was a mop and in the other a plastic bag with what looked like cleaning supplies. "Hi. Who's that outside with Nick?"

Claire stared. "I don't know. What are you doing here?"

Lori smiled and lifted her hands, showing off her items like trophies. "Came to clean. Sandy will be by later to help and I think Peggy said she'd stop in, too."

Claire shook her head. "You don't have to do this."

Lori lowered her arms. "I know I don't *have* to. I *want* to." She set the supplies down. "But first I want to know who that handsome man outside with Nick is."

Disconcerted by Lori's insistence, Claire followed her out into the afternoon sunshine. The warm air felt wonderful against her face. The clean scent of the lilac bush was a welcome reprieve from the smell of smoke. They followed the sound of voices to the back of The Zone. Nick stood a head or so taller than the Latino-looking man who introduced himself as Mario Benitto, the claims adjuster from her insurance company.

"Thank you for coming so quickly," Claire said politely, shooting Nick a curious glance. Why hadn't Nick informed her the man had arrived?

Lori nudged Claire in the side. "What?"

Lori gave her a pointed look.

"Oh." Amused, Claire said, "This is Lori Pearson."

The man smiled, showing white teeth as he extended his hand to Lori. "It's a pleasure to meet you."

Lori made a little noise in her throat. "Pleasure's all mine," she murmured beneath her breath.

Mario's eyes crinkled at the corners with good humor. Claire had the distinct impression he'd heard Lori's comment. The claims adjuster turned his light brown gaze to her. "I'll write up my report and send over the paperwork for you to sign."

"Oh. Okay."

Mario turned to Nick and the men shook hands.

"Ladies." Mario tipped his head with a smile that included Claire but his interest was clearly on Lori.

As soon as the man's car pulled away from the curb, Claire planted her hands on her hips and faced Nick. "Why didn't you come get me when he arrived?"

He drew his brows together. "I was just trying to help."

"You were trying to take over. This is my responsibility. I'm capable of dealing with the insurance company."

He held up a hand. "I didn't mean to step on your toes."

Lori backed up a step. "I'll just be inside." She hurried away.

"I'm glad to see you've got help," Nick commented quietly.

"I didn't ask her to come. She just showed up," Claire said quickly.

"I'm just saying, it's good of you to bless her by letting her help."

She tucked in her chin. "Bless her?"

His expression softened. His mouth curved up on one side. "Yes, bless her. 'It is more blessed to give than to receive.' She's given you her time and her energy. Don't rob her of her blessing."

Claire pondered his words. "So, you're saying I'm robbing you of your blessing if I don't let you help?" she asked slowly.

He raised a cocky brow. "Yes. That's what I'm saying."

She rolled her eyes. "I hate it when people quote Scripture to further their own agenda."

His expression turned contrite. "Look, Claire. I figured since you'd hired me to do the work, I should be the one to explain to the guy what needed to be done. I really didn't mean to upset you."

What he said made sense. Her initial indignation faded in the face of his sincere words. "I'm sorry I got upset. I'm so used to doing everything myself that I…"

"Have trouble giving up control?" he finished.

A wry laugh burst from her. "That pretty much sums it up."

She sobered and stared into his dark eyes, seeing kindness and understanding.

"There's no shame in asking for help."

She nodded, feeling herself lost in his gaze. "I guess I should go help Lori," she muttered.

"Probably."

But neither moved. Claire felt drawn to him and warning bells went off in her head. There was something about this man that lured her to him as if he were a bug light and she were some fluttery insect. Only she wasn't about to get close enough to get zapped. She knew up front this one was leaving. She backed away.

"Claire?"

Her name on his lips sent waves of warmth through her. "Yeah?"

"I've an errand to run. Can I borrow your car?"

"Oh, sure. Anytime." Then she hurried for the safety of The Zone.

Nick drove slowly through the side streets of Pineridge, his gaze alert and searching for the three errant teens. The runaways.

The tree-lined streets were quiet. The houses with their well-kept yards, a minivan here or an SUV there, all whispered tranquillity. Tranquillity he'd never get a chance to know, now that Serena was gone.

People who were in their yards or on their porches usually stopped whatever they were doing to watch him drive by—some stared with mild curiosity while others with wary suspicion.

He'd become used to the second type in the last two years—a man on a Harley attracted attention. Interest from some, mostly females, but the majority felt suspicion. So what was it about him in a green hatchback? He tightened his grip around the steering wheel of Claire's car and headed away from the nice suburban neighborhoods to more commercial areas.

He'd already stopped by the police department and had a word with Officer Bob. Bob had assured him the police were still looking for the teens, but without evidence there wasn't much they could do beyond keeping an eye on them.

Nick cruised into an industrial park bordered on either side by typical Oregon woods. Tall trees and thick underbrush. A hundred feet down the way, a boy emerged from between two buildings.

The blond kid from the park!

Nick sped up. The boy froze for a split second and then took off at a dead run through the dusty parking lot where he veered off into the thick woods. Nick threw the car's transmission into park, jumped out and took up the chase.

He crashed through the trees, but the kid had disappeared. Nick stopped. Bending at the waist, he braced his hands on his knees as he listened for noise to direct his search.

In the distance the faint hum of traffic underlined the sounds of the woods. A bird chirped to his left. The clickity-clack of a squirrel's nails as it climbed the bark of a nearby tree echoed through the woods. The faint rustling of leaves stirred by the slight breeze taunted him.

Nick straightened and made his way out of the trees. Back in the car, he drove around the buildings, looking for likely places the teens would hang out. On the backside of the lot several of the buildings were empty and boarded up.

There were any number of places for three runaways to hide.

Nick left, deciding he'd come back later, after dark. Because he didn't need proof that the kids had started the fire. His gut told him they had and he'd make sure the punks paid.

He owed that much to Claire.

Chapter Six

When Nick arrived at The Zone, Claire and Little Nick were playing in the front yard with a small rubber ball.

"Look, he fetches," she exclaimed with a big smile that lit her whole face.

"That's great," Nick replied, but his gaze never strayed off Claire.

She'd changed into a summery dress with little strappy sandals that allowed her pink-tipped toes to peek out. Her sleek blond hair was parted on one side and held back by a fancy clip.

She looked young and fresh, but the sparkle of wonder in her eyes lodged a knot in his throat. It called to a part of him he'd buried beneath so much bitterness he'd almost forgotten wonder and awe existed.

Shaken, he sat on the stair beside her. "Have you ever had a dog?"

She shook her head. "Aunt Denise had cats. What about you?"

He laughed, remembering. "My sister and I had an assortment of pets through the years. Dogs, cats, guinea pigs, rats. A python that drove my mother to hysterics. We once had a tortoise named Speedy."

Her interested gaze trapped his. "That's so cool. One of Aunt Denise's cats had kittens and she let me keep one. A black ball of fur that slept on my pillow until we realized I was allergic to cats. All watery eyes and runny nose. It wasn't pretty."

He shared her chuckle, though he couldn't imagine her not looking pretty. "What happened to your aunt?"

Claire's small, slender hands smoothed her skirt over her knees. "She died of lymphoma."

He covered her restless hands. "I'm sorry."

"Thank you."

"How old were you?" He rubbed the back of her warm hand with his thumb.

"Just finishing my last year of college. It's been two years now."

The same amount of time since he'd lost Serena. They shared the connection of having lost someone they loved. His heart throbbed. "Was she sick long?"

"No. It hit fast." She extracted her hand and stood. "Are you hungry?"

He pushed himself off the stair, acknowledging her need to change the subject. He felt the same. "Yes, food would be great. Leftover pizza?"

For some reason she flushed. "Uh, no, uh, I was thinking…maybe Chinese tonight. Or we could go to the hamburger joint where Gwen waitresses."

"Whichever."

She scooped up the puppy and hurried inside.

Nick waited on the steps. He scanned the park across the street even as he told himself to keep a distance from his very pretty and sweet hostess.

Over the next few days, Claire watched with equal doses of amazement and annoyance as Nick took charge of the men who'd volunteered their labor. He organized and smoothly created a team effort. They'd brought in equipment and lumber. The back of The Zone was dismantled and the frame for the new door was up.

After their conversation about the insurance company, Claire allowed Nick to handle the situation. She signed where he'd indicated and appreciated the way he kept her informed. She'd struggled with letting him take charge, but she was smart enough to acknowledge he was doing a great job.

Unfortunately, she hadn't done a bang-up job of getting inside his head. Whenever they were alone and she had the opportunity to find out more about him, she felt tongue-tied and scattered. She had to get a grip.

Today, she vowed, would be different.

The day was sunny. Perfect Oregon weather. The kind that made unsuspecting people want to move to the state. Only, when the rain hit for days on end, they'd soon realize how precious and rare the sunny days were.

She found Nick in the back, using a power saw to cut boards. She sat on the grass. Little Nick chewed on a toy at her feet.

Nick had taken off his shirt, revealing long, lean muscles beneath tanned skin. His beauty was distracting. She'd sought him out for a reason, but she hesitated to speak for fear she'd startle him. Saws made her nervous. All that noise. That sharp blade.

"You having a good day?" he asked without turning, effectively dismissing her fear that she'd distract him.

"I am. You've done a wonderful job so far."

"Wasn't just me."

"I know." He was so quick to give credit away. She liked that. "How come you know so much about building and things?"

He lowered the board he was cutting and went to the pile of lumber. He picked up several, discarded them and then finally settled on one, which he took to the saw. "My father owns a hardware and lumber store," he finally answered.

She smiled at his back. "On Long Island?"

"That's right. It started out a real mom-and-pop operation, but he's expanded. Some of the big conglomerates have offered to buy him out because he has a great location for the area. But he's not ready to retire. Mom's ready for him to, though. She'd like to travel, but the business is Dad's baby. He's devoted his whole life to making it a success."

"At your expense?" she ventured, wondering if that was the deep hurt she sensed in him.

His glance was razor sharp. "No. He's a great dad. To both me and my sister."

Envy twisted inside her. Ugly and dark. She envied him that his parents were still together and that he thought his father had been a good dad. She envied that he had a sibling. Someone to confide in, share childhood memories with. She envied that he had family to love. "What's your sister's name?"

"Lucy. She's a fireball just like her namesake, Lucille Ball. My mom really liked the Lucy and Desi show. I'm lucky they didn't name me Desi." He finished with the board, laid it on the ground next to the others, and then turned off the saw.

"Were you named after someone?"

He nodded as he came to sit beside her. "After my grandfather, on my mom's side."

"Did you know your grandfather?"

"Sure." He slanted her a glance. "Didn't you know your grandparents?"

Claire shook her head. "My mom's parents live in Arizona. I saw them once when I was ten, but they weren't real warm people. And my dad and Aunt Denise's parents passed away when I was a baby."

"What happened to your parents?"

She took a deep breath. "My parents divorced when I was twelve and I came to live with Aunt Denise."

Nick noticed the strained tone of her voice. "Why not with one of your parents?"

She plucked at the grass. "Just didn't."

Did that mean neither of her parents had wanted her? Or she hadn't wanted them? Nick's chest tightened. "I'm sorry. That must have been tough, being away from both parents."

"I suppose," she said noncommittedly.

The sadness in her eyes cried out to his soul. He didn't want to take on her pain, too.

The silence stretched. His curiosity got the better of him. "Did you grow up here, Claire?"

"No."

"Where?"

"Portland," she said finally.

"Are both your parents still there?"

"My dad died in an accident on the job the year I graduated from high school." She lifted a shoulder in a careless gesture. "Don't know about my mother."

He turned to fully face her. "I'm sorry for your loss. You don't have contact with your mother?"

"Nope," she said, a bit too cheery. "It's for the best."

"How can not having contact with your mother be for the best?" He stared at her intently. "Is it your choice not to see her?"

She was tempted to look away, but instead unflinchingly held his gaze. "At first it was, but then after my father died, I contacted her. We talked on the phone and she made it clear there was no room in her life for me. She asked me not to contact her again."

She cleared her throat, hating how her mother's rejection still hurt. "Now, you know about my family. I'd much rather hear about yours." She could see he wanted to press, but she headed off his unspoken questions with a question of her own. "You're close with your grandfather?"

His mouth quirked at the corner. "All my grandparents, actually. The whole family, both sides, gathers every Sunday after church for dinner at our house."

"They *all* live on Long Island?" she asked.

He nodded. "Pretty much. Two sets of grandparents, aunts and uncles, tons of cousins. I lived in Manhattan for years, but always came home for the weekends."

She couldn't fathom that. "Do you miss your family?"

A dark shadow flickered in his eyes. "I do."

Her earlier suspicion was on target. His pain definitely had something to do with his family. "When was the last time you saw them?"

His gaze slid away. "A year and a half ago."

"That's a long time."

He grunted.

"Did you come out west for a job or something?"

His expression closed. He gave a negative shake of his head.

"What made you leave?" she probed.

What could drive such a steadfast and determined man away from the family he obviously adored? If she'd had parents like that, a family…she pushed the dark thought away.

"It's complicated. My parents wanted me to take over the hardware store. I couldn't do that."

"Ah. Bigger aspirations?"

He frowned. "Don't get me wrong. The business is great. For my dad. I had different dreams."

"What are your dreams?"

When his gaze came back to her, she sucked in a breath at the guarded expression darkening his eyes. "I'm not going there, Claire."

He'd set a boundary, she respected that. But still…

Realization struck with lightning-bright clarity. He was a grown-up runaway. God had brought him to her for a reason. He had saved her so she could save him. She liked a good challenge. "Does your family even know where you are?"

With one hand he rubbed at his neck. "I drop them a line once in awhile."

"Did you have a fight, is that why you left?" she pressed.

Blatantly ignoring her question, he stood and picked up the cut boards, his muscles bunching in a fascinating way. He carried the boards to the side of the building, leaving her alone.

She picked a blade of grass and split it in the middle. Nick's refusal to follow in his father's footsteps would obviously divide a family.

Aunt Denise used to say a family was only as strong as the threads binding them. Nick had said he missed them. That they were good parents. By the sound of it, he had a close-knit family. Nick's threads were weakened, but not severed, which gave her hope that the bond could be strengthened. If she could convince him to contact his parents, the haunted look might leave his eyes.

And she'd have the satisfaction of knowing she'd helped him do something she'd been unable to do for herself.

Two days later, Nick returned from an early morning walk around the perimeters of The Zone looking for any evidence that the kids had returned. The empty lots on either side of The Zone's boundaries showed no signs of disturbance. So far his search for the teens hadn't yielded much.

Just that one brief glimpse of the blond kid.

Nick had gone back to the warehouses several times, but to no avail. He'd look downtown again today. The teens had to surface at some point, unless they'd left town. One could hope.

His stomach clenched at the sight of Claire coming down the walkway from the front of The Zone. The heels of her brown sandals clicked on the cement. An ankle-length denim skirt covered her long legs.

The blue tank showed off her slender arms and graceful neck. Her blond hair shimmered in the afternoon sun. He hadn't noticed before the streaks of red highlights, making her more strawberry blond.

In her hands, she carried a brown leather purse and a hooded gray sweatjacket. She really was very lovely. He liked that she didn't feel the need to hide behind layers of makeup and overly styled hair.

"Where are you headed?" Nick asked.

She turned her head, sending her hair sliding across her shoulders. "I'm going to the bank."

"Anything I could help with?"

For a moment there was eagerness in her eyes, but she quickly shook her head. "I've got everything under control."

And there it was. She liked being in control of her life to the point that accepting, let alone asking for help, was seen as some kind of weakness. It made Nick sad to think she lived her life so self-confined.

"Mind if I walk with you?" He fell in step with her. "I want to check on my bike."

She relaxed, a teasing light appeared in her clear eyes. "Miss riding out on the open road?"

He made a noncommittal noise.

Strangely, he wasn't missing the "open road." He attributed the lack of restlessness to the distraction of rebuilding the back of The Zone. Once he was finished he was certain his memories and pain would push him on.

They walked through the park and down the main street. He enjoyed the companionable way she chatted about what she'd seen on the local news channel that morning. It felt natural to be with her as if they'd known each other for a long time.

As they passed by the hardware store, the owner, Mr. Hanson, waved a greeting to Nick through the window. They'd struck up a friendship once the older man had realized how much Nick knew about hardware and carpentry. Mr. Hanson had even offered Nick a job, much to Nick's amusement.

Nick didn't need a job or money. At least not yet. He'd made wise choices in the stock market for both himself and his clients before Serena's death. And after…he'd sold or given away everything they'd had. He lived off the interest in his bank account.

A fat lot of good that was to his empty heart.

As Nick and Claire approached the open door of Tessa's Bakery, Nick slowed and touched Claire's arm to indicate he wanted to go in. The spicy smell of cinnamon bread that mingled with the sweet scent of pastries made his mouth water, but the response seemed mild compared to the way his pulse jumped when Claire smiled her approval of their unexpected stop.

Tessa Burke came to the counter as they stepped inside. She was a slightly plump woman in her early fifties, with a wide smile and twinkling gray eyes. "How are you two today?"

"Good, thanks." Nick helped himself to a sample of cinnamon bread. "How's Timmy?" Tessa had told Nick all about her grandson during an earlier visit.

Tessa's eyes lit up. "He's great. Thank you for asking. He turns four next week."

"Wow, four. That's a milestone." Nick handed Claire a piece of bread.

As she took the morsel from him, her fingers brushed his, the contact almost causing him to drop the bread before she fully had hold of it. She popped the piece in her mouth and made an approving sound. "This is delicious, Tessa."

The woman beamed. "This was one of your aunt's favorites."

"I remember," Claire stated as she snagged another piece off the platter on the counter.

"Could we have a loaf to go?" Nick slanted Claire a grin. "Breakfast."

She grinned back, her blue eyes twinkling. She nodded eagerly. He paid for the bread before they moved on.

They stopped at the foot of the concrete stairs leading into the bank. The large white square structure was impressive in its beauty. Tall white pillars flanked the double brass-framed doors. Multiple flower baskets hung from hooks along the overhang shielding the doorway from the elements.

"Sure you don't want me to come with you?" Nick asked as he propped a hip on the railing.

She waved her hand. "No, no. I wouldn't want to keep you from your bike."

With a little shock, he realized he'd been so engrossed in Claire's company that he'd forgotten to stop at the mechanic's shop. "I'm where I want to be."

She backed up a few steps. The sun cast shadows on her face, hiding her eyes. "I need to go in now."

"I'll see you later."

She turned and fled to the building.

He certainly was treading in dangerous water.

Claire finished her business at the bank and walked outside into the sunshine. She glanced around and chided herself for the little bubble of disappointment that Nick wasn't here waiting for her. She would have liked one of his strong shoulders to cry on, though she doubted she would have said anything had he really been waiting. She knew better than to look for comfort from others.

It had rankled her sense of self-sufficiency to ask the bank manager for an extension on her loan payments, only to be told politely, but firmly, no. Her stomach dropped. Somehow she needed to figure out a way to squeeze more money from her budget.

She walked down a side street behind the library and stopped at the small patch of grass with a picnic bench beneath a large old oak tree. Today the spot was empty, but this was one place the teens in town sometimes hung out. The place she and Mindy had agreed upon as a place for them to communicate with each other.

Claire pulled out a sheet of paper from her purse and wrote a note on it. She folded the paper into a small square and stuck the note in the pocket of the gray hooded sweatjacket she'd brought from her closet before laying the jacket on the table.

"Lord, make sure Mindy gets this, please."

Knowing she couldn't do any more for now, she headed toward Main Street.

Nick would be at The Zone by now. She was glad he hadn't asked any more questions about her need to help the teenagers. She didn't know why she was so reluctant to tell him. She'd dealt with it all during college. She'd have been hard pressed not to earn a degree in counseling without coming to terms with her own life.

Maybe she was afraid he'd look at her with the same disgust with which he'd looked at Tyler and Mindy. The same look her parents had worn the last time she'd seen them face-to-face.

No, keeping Nick in the dark about why she felt such a kinship with the teens was for the best. She needed to guard her heart and her past by keeping Nick at a distance.

From the hardware store's front window, Nick saw Claire round the corner from the side of the library and head back down Main Street. He hoped her meeting had gone well, but the pensive expression on her lovely face concerned him.

A fierce protectiveness grabbed hold of him with

stunning intensity. He hated the thought of Claire suffering. Past or present. Hated more the idea that she'd suffer in the future. A certainty if she stayed on her present course.

He wasn't necessarily opposed to her idea of a teen shelter. In theory, The Zone could work. But for one lone woman to take on such a burden…it would only result in heartache for Claire. She was a woman who gave without conditions, without reservations.

An easy mark.

He felt the need to protect her not only physically, but also emotionally, which was a really bad thing, considering he didn't want to be responsible for anyone.

He'd do what he could before he left, but he had a feeling he was digging himself a hole.

Though at the moment, he needed her opinion about paint color for The Zone. Setting the paint supplies he'd gathered on the counter, he told the clerk he'd be right back and then headed out of the store to intercept Claire.

"Hey, beautiful," he said as he came alongside her.

She halted and her head jerked up. "Nick, you startled me."

"You were lost in thought."

Her pink lips curved into a half smile. "That's me, always thinking."

"Good thoughts, I hope."

Her eyes widened slightly, a faint reddish tinge colored her cheeks. She shifted her purse from one slim shoulder to the other. "Oh, you know. Just random thoughts."

He cocked his head. "Didn't you have a jacket with you earlier?"

She dropped her gaze and tucked a stray strand of hair behind her ear. "I…uh, left my jacket somewhere."

"Do you want some help finding it?"

She gave a small laugh. "No. I'm sure it's fine. Are you headed back to The Zone?"

"In a while. How'd it go at the bank?"

The corners of her pretty mouth tipped down. "Not as well as planned."

"What's going on? Can I help?"

Uncertainty crept into her expression. "I…" She shook her head and the uncertainty left. In its place was proud determination. "I'll manage. Just a little glitch."

He scratched his chin with his knuckle, trying to keep hold of his frustration. Her independence was a hindrance to anyone trying to get close to her, though he doubted she'd take kindly to that observation or agree with his assessment. Which he shouldn't be making in the first place. He didn't want to get close to her. "Would you help me match the color of paint for The Zone?"

Her eyes widened. "You're ready to paint?"

"Not quite, but I'd like to have everything gathered before we're ready to start."

At the hardware store, Nick led her to the paint aisle. Claire picked up one swatch after another, comparing colors and shades to the sample of The

Zone's paint that Nick had brought with him. Finally, she settled on one. "This looks as close as we're going to get." She handed him the swatch.

His fingers closed around it and her hand. Their gazes met over the color swatch.

The flare of attraction ignited. He knew she felt it, too.

The longing and trepidation in her eyes tore at him. A deep ache welled up inside of him, urging him to pull her into his arms and chase away whatever driving force kept her so closed off. He tugged on her hand, drawing her near, and her eyes widened. But then, like a shade being drawn, her expression became remote, distant. He remembered Lori's words. A wall had definitely just gone up.

With polite gracefulness she extracted her hand. "I have work to do. I'm sure I'll see you later."

She walked out of the store. Nick stared after her, tempted to follow, but he stayed rooted to the floor. He was definitely digging himself in.

He just hoped he didn't dig so deep he couldn't get back out.

Chapter Seven

An hour later, as Nick left the hardware store, a figure emerging from around the corner of the library at the far end of Main Street grabbed his attention. The girl he'd first seen Claire with—Mindy, if he remembered correctly—stepped out onto the sidewalk. She seemed to be searching for someone. She had on the same jeans as before but she also sported a gray hooded jacket that looked familiar.

With one hand, he scratched his chin, the bristles of the day's growth of whiskers rasping roughly against his calloused fingers. That jacket.

In his mind an image of Claire flashed like a slide show. Her walking downtown, her long skirt brushing her trim ankles with a gray jacket tucked under her arm. Then later coming back from her appointment without the jacket.

Now Mindy had the jacket. He fisted his hands. Had she stolen from Claire? But when and how? At the bank?

I left it somewhere.

No. Claire had given it to the girl. Probably when Claire had been behind the library. She was still trying to protect them.

Nick hefted his supplies in his arms, partially covering his face, yet not so much that he couldn't see Mindy. He decided to follow her. See if she led him to the ringleader. Tyler.

Mindy started walking up the street. Nick walked parallel to her on the opposite side of the wide road. She didn't seem to be in a hurry. When she came to a garbage can on the corner of Main and Elm, she paused.

Nick stopped and, still using his bag of supplies for cover, pretended to study the newspaper stand.

Mindy leaned against the can. Her gaze shifting quickly side to side before she turned and reached inside the can. He frowned. What was she doing?

She grabbed something out of the can before hurrying down the side street with her prize. Nick quickly crossed the street, but by the time he got to the corner of Elm she'd disappeared.

He spun around and his gaze went directly to the garbage can. He stalked over to it and peered inside. A sick feeling descended over him, weighing him down.

He backed away and swiped a hand over his eyes as if he could wipe away the image of what he'd witnessed. It wasn't as if he'd never seen a homeless person take from the garbage. He'd lived in New York long enough to see many awful things. He'd ridden through enough other big cities to know how common homelessness was.

But never before had he felt anything.

He wouldn't think about what the girl had taken. It didn't matter. He wouldn't let compassion get to him.

Claire heard the front door open and close. Gwen was already up in her room studying, so it could only be Nick. The heavy, masculine footsteps going up the stairs confirmed that thought. She sat at her desk in her office, the financial records and budget proposal for The Zone spread out before her across the oak desktop.

Everything inside her stilled as she listened to Nick come back down the stairs.

Usually they ate dinner together. Take-out or sandwiches. Sometimes heading to the restaurant where Gwen worked. Claire really did enjoyed Nick's company, but tonight she'd felt too vulnerable with the pressure of her visit to the bank to dine with him. She'd been glad when he'd said Dave, Steve and the man she hadn't recognized, Gary Parks, were going out for dinner and wanted him to join them.

She'd needed to distance herself, control the urge to confide in him.

The footsteps stopped outside the office door, then she heard a soft knock.

"Yes?" she called.

"Are you okay?" His voice sounded concerned.

She smiled at the door. "Yes, thank you."

"I brought you something."

Curious, she untucked her bare feet from beneath her and padded across the hardwood floor. She opened the door. The light spilling out from her office cast shadows across Nick's tall form. In his hand he held a white bag.

"I didn't know if you'd eaten, but I brought you some pasta from Cannelli's."

His thoughtfulness touched her deeply. "That was sweet of you. Did you have a good time?"

"Yes, actually." He said it like he was surprised that he'd enjoyed himself. "We played darts, ate tons of food. It was a really good time."

He was making connections and she was pleased. Maybe soon he'd realize he needed to reconnect with his family.

He held out the bag. "Are you hungry?"

"Yes. I am."

She took the bag and opened it. The delicious aroma of basil and garlic wafted out from the foam container. There was even a fork and napkins in the bag. Her stomach grumbled its appreciation.

Nick chuckled.

She glanced up with a sheepish grin. "This smells great."

"Go ahead, eat."

She moved past him and sat on the bottom stair, then pulled everything out of the bag and laid it on her lap and said a prayer of thanks. She picked up the fork, ready to take a bite when she sensed Nick's studied gaze. He leaned against the open doorjamb of her office, his arms crossed over his chest. She froze. "What?"

His brows came together. "I saw Mindy today wearing your jacket."

Her pulse gave a leap and her heart smiled. God had made sure she received the jacket. That was good. "Did you?"

He eyed her, clearly not buying her innocent act. "What is it with you and those kids?"

"I have to build their trust somehow. One step at a time."

He scoffed. "You make it sound like you're trying to tame a wild animal."

"I've never thought of it that way, but yeah, I suppose. Each kid is different. It's tricky gauging what strategy to use."

"Have you worked with kids before now? Besides Gwen."

"I was a Young Life leader during college and I volunteered at a shelter in Portland."

"Is that where you met Gwen?"

She nodded. "Aunt Denise and I stumbled over her, literally."

"Is that what prompted you to open a shelter?"

She ducked her head. "Among other things."

He looked toward her desk. "What are you working on?"

She grimaced. "Trying to work up a feasible projected budget for The Zone."

"Having trouble?"

She made a face. "I never was any good with math, but I'm muddling through it."

"Let me look at them." He disappeared into the office.

She scrambled to her feet, leaving her food on the stairs, and hurried to his side at her desk.

Against the backdrop of her white walls, he was a splash of life and color in denim and a green-striped button-down shirt. She blinked, trying to rein in her galloping heart. He invaded her space. Crowded her senses.

He picked up one sheet of paper from the desk and studied it before turning to another. He sank down on her white wicker desk-chair. It squeaked beneath his weight. He seemed to lose himself in the papers, so she retrieved her food and sat on the short bench that she'd pushed up against the wall.

"Who are these budgets for?" he asked, finally.

She stopped chewing and quickly swallowed. "Well, I'm hoping to put together proposals for grant money. Someone suggested that would be the best way to raise funds."

Nick turned to look at her. "How have you raised funds so far?"

"Mostly word of mouth. Mainly, Sandy and Dave's mouths."

Nick didn't doubt that the couple would do all they could to help Claire even if she didn't want them to. He didn't envy the battle they must fight every time they tried. "They care about you."

She shifted on the bench, looking uncomfortable. "Sandy and my aunt were best friends."

He narrowed his gaze. "So you think they care because they feel obligated?"

Her chin rose, her gaze direct. "Why else would they?"

"Because *you,* Claire Wilcox, are a generous, caring woman."

A blush like a shadow crossed over her pale complexion. He watched her tidy up, putting the barely touched foam container back in the bag, folding the top of the bag over, her hands toying with the edge. It saddened him that she couldn't accept a simple compliment.

Okay. Not so simple considering she hardly knew him. He slowly began to notice his surroundings. The walls were stark white. The oak desk and the matching oak bench the only furniture. His gaze landed on the two pictures on the wall.

Angels. Beautiful creatures in charcoal drawings. He got up and moved closer to inspect one. There in the corner he read the signature of the artist, C. Wilcox. He smiled with amazement. "You did these?"

When she didn't answer, he turned around. She abruptly rose and stood in the middle of her small office. Her hands clutched the white bag. He could see her mentally withdrawing as she looked at him warily. "Just doodlings that Aunt Denise framed. It seemed a shame to throw them away when she'd put so much effort in framing them."

"They're wonderful," he said. He came to stand in front of her. "Don't sell yourself so short." He didn't mean for his words to sound as harsh as they did.

She drew herself up. "Thank you for dinner. You must be tired after working so hard all day. I won't keep you."

Nick fisted his hands in frustration. She was shutting him out again, keeping herself self-contained, closed off. He really shouldn't care.

"Walls imprison as well as protect, Claire."

She pressed her lips into a tight line.

Irked by her stubbornness, he stalked back to her desk and breathed deep to clear the irritation from his brain. His fists relaxed. He crossed his arms over his chest as he turned to face her, ready to meet the battle head-on.

"Would it be too much to ask for you to let me help with this?" He gestured with his head toward her desk. This was something he was good at. Something he could do for her that wouldn't further his attraction or the ridiculous need to break through her icy walls.

She pulled her lip between her slightly crooked teeth. "You don't have to. I can manage."

He gathered his patience. "I know you can manage. It would make *me* feel good to help you."

She blinked and cocked her head to one side as if weighing the truth of his words. "Really?"

He remembered their conversation earlier in the week. He'd told her it blessed others to give their help. She'd accused him of using Scripture to further his own agenda. He didn't have an agenda. "Yes, really."

"You know about budgets and stuff?"

He unfolded his arms and hitched a hip on the edge of the desk. At least she hadn't flat-out said no. "I know budgets and stuff."

Humor danced in her eyes and she visibly relaxed. "A man of many talents."

"Jack-of-all-trades."

She laughed. The deep throaty sound wrapped

around him, teasing his senses, making him want to make her laugh again.

"Okay." She made a sweeping gesture with her hand. "Be my guest."

Scrambling to control the chaos inside of him, he sat down at her desk. He forced his concentration on the papers in front of him, though he was acutely aware of the woman staring over his shoulder.

Claire didn't know what to make of the feelings bouncing around her head and her heart. She felt like she'd been outwitted by the sincerity in his plea to let him help her. Every time she turned around, Nick was working his way under her guard. Or, according to him, the walls she had erected around herself. Ha! If he only knew what protection those walls afforded her.

A blessing, he'd said before.

But asking for help, accepting help, threatened her vow of self-sufficiency.

Yet, she wasn't feeling threatened. It kind of felt good to think he'd wanted to help her. That he would receive some pleasure or a blessing from doing so.

He dwarfed her little oak desk and wicker chair. His dark hair fell forward as he bent over the pages. His hand holding the pencil deftly manipulated the numbers. She peered over his shoulder, amazed by the way he brought the numbers to life.

"You know, this would be a lot easier if you had a computer," he said.

She pulled a face. "I know. It's on my to-do list."

He grunted and returned his focus to the papers

in front of him. He asked questions. Wanted to see her bill statements and know what her expenditures were. She should have felt like he was invading her privacy, but she didn't. She gladly handed him any information he wanted. She couldn't believe how much time and energy he was saving her. She almost felt bad for using him so shamelessly.

Pulling out another file folder full of paperwork from the cardboard box that served as a file cabinet, she explained to him about the nightmare of laws and regulations and agencies she'd been dealing with and still dealt with. "Often one agency's require-ments conflict with another's. But different agencies have different concerns."

He flipped through the pages and whistled through his teeth. "Wow, how do you keep it all straight?"

She shrugged. "You're looking at my file sys-tem."

He turned in the chair, hooking one arm over the back. "We need to perk up your office space a bit. A computer with Excel, a real filing cabinet, stackable file holders."

She pointed to the papers on the desk. "Put that in the budget."

His mouth quirked up. "What about staffing? Do you plan to hire help? And how many?"

She sighed. "Staffing is regulated by minimum licensing standards. Which is another headache. Eventually, I'll have to hire more workers. There's a minimum staff to client ratio. I don't need to worry about that until closer to the official opening.

So for now, it's just me, but I don't plan on taking a paycheck."

He held up a hand. "You should take a paycheck."

"I'm not in this for profit," she argued. She wanted to help the teenagers, not make money off them.

His brows drew down. "I'm not talking profit. I'm talking about personal items that you won't be able to write off as business expenses."

"Oh." She twirled a lock of hair around her finger. "I never thought of that."

"So what other hurdles do you have to jump?"

He sounded interested and she willed her mind to work as she fell into his compelling gaze. "The facility must meet specific standards for a group home. I'll have to run through the hoops to meet the fire codes again after the repairs. I was planning on opening the doors at the beginning of July, but now, I'm thinking August."

He nodded encouragingly.

She continued. "And then there's funding. Thus the need for a feasible budget. Achieving nonprofit status helps because I can solicit donations and apply for grants."

His eyes lighted up. "I know about grants. For the proposals, you'll need to come up with a mission statement. Do you have one?"

Claire tucked in her chin. "Not off the top of my head."

He waved his hand. "Not a problem. We'll come up with something, preferably fifty words or less. The foundations you apply to will want a copy of your proposed budget and they'll want to know what specifically the money is for. Some foundations won't give money for operating expenses. They don't want the recipient to rely on them for their cash flow. Most corporations like to see the fruit of the donation, something tangible, which could be anything from computers to an art teacher. Or maybe in the case of The Zone, a shrink or a zookeeper."

"Hey, wait a second," she protested, her defenses kicking in. But then she saw the teasing glint in his eyes. "You," she huffed with a smile, liking that he teased her. Liking *him*.

His grin packed a high voltage punch.

Her stomach cartwheeled, and her heart added a few extra beats, emphasizing the effect he had on her. It wasn't just his looks that kicked her senses into high gear. There was a kindness in his dark eyes when he looked at her that made her feel special. She hadn't felt special in a long time.

Mentally kicking herself, she dropped her gaze to the desktop. She wouldn't get sucked in by this man. She just wouldn't.

"How do you know so much about grant writing?"

"My..." he paused, his hands stalling in the act of writing. "I knew someone who worked for a non-profit ministry. I helped her write grants."

A twinge of jealousy for some unknown "her" assaulted Claire's senses. Of course, there'd been a "her." Probably a long line of them considering he was handsome and kind, a man full of honor. A man worth wanting.

She wasn't looking for a man. But if she were, Nick would fill the bill.

"Where are these from?" He flicked the tassels hanging from her lamp.

"The black-and-blue one is from Pineridge High, and the green and yellow from U of O." At his questioning look, she clarified. "University of Oregon." She held up a fist and pumped it. "Go Ducks."

"Ducks?"

"Hey, it's Oregon, the wettest state in the Union. We have Ducks and Beavers. And believe me, the two camps are divided with a deep rivalry."

"Did you live off campus or in the dorm?"

"Started in the dorm, but it was too…" she trailed off, unsure how to describe the close quarters, the girls with their boyfriends and their parents who cared. The loneliness. "I never really fit in."

"I didn't like the dorm life much, either," he said. "Too many people wanting to know where I was going, what I was doing. The parties were fun the first year or so but after that it became tedious."

She nodded. "I went to a few parties that first year." Did things she'd rather forget. "After that, I decided to get serious about school."

"It's paid off." He showed her his calculations. "I'm impressed, Claire," he declared. "You've done a really good job of accomplishing so much with such a small budget."

His praise warmed her battered soul like heat from a bonfire in the middle of winter.

She was impressed, too. He certainly knew what he was doing. There was more to this man than met the eye. "What school did you attend?"

"Columbia."

Very prestigious. "What was your major?"

"Economics."

"Ah. That's why you know so much about budgets. So, what did you do after school?"

He looked uncomfortable. "I worked on Wall Street for a brokerage firm."

She frowned, trying to put all the pieces together. "You worked on Wall Street, but your parents were pressuring you to come in to the family business?"

She couldn't decipher what she saw in his dark eyes. "No. My parents were proud of me. It wasn't until later that Dad asked me to come work with him."

"Later?"

He gave her an odd, guarded look, then glanced at the black leather watch on his wrist. "It's late. I should let you get your rest."

Her first impression of him as the bad boy on a Harley was being radically changed, yet she wasn't losing interest. Quite the opposite.

And that scared her.

Deep into the night, Nick lay stretched out on the too-short twin mattress trying to doze off. His mind was abuzz with admiration for Claire. Her dedication was over-the-top. She'd managed the funds she'd been responsible for so far. She'd made every penny count, had documented every gift and donation, which helped to determine The Zone's budget.

He shifted on the bed, trying for a more comfortable position. He didn't really mind being uncomfortable, though. Not if it meant keeping Claire safe.

Though he didn't know if he was going to be able

to keep *himself* safe from Claire. He was confident he could control his attraction to her. But her curious mind was always working. Probing. He saw the way she studied him after he'd told her about working on Wall Street. Like he were some intricate puzzle that she was determined to solve.

But the worse part was he'd almost told her about Serena.

Telling her would serve no purpose. Telling her would only stir up his pain.

A noise echoed in the quiet of his room. He stilled, listening. It was Claire again.

He glanced at the clock. 3:00 a.m. Right on schedule. Most nights she got up, walked past his room and went downstairs for a few hours. At first he'd thought it was for the puppy, but after the second night, Little Nick had been tucked into his crate before she'd gone to bed.

He sat up. He should go check on her, make sure she was okay. He didn't—it was too dangerous an endeavor.

So instead he prayed for her. And for himself. All the while hoping, but not really believing, that God would listen to him.

Chapter Eight

Claire paused outside Nick's door on Sunday morning. Her heart picked up speed and she suddenly felt shy and exposed. The man on the other side of the door was so much more than she'd ever expected or experienced.

He was fun and nice. She found his wry sense of humor enticing. His sharp wit and intelligence challenged her. There was so much to like about him. So, so much to be afraid of.

She strove for the indifference that had served her well over the years. She couldn't let herself care for a man who obviously disliked the kids she'd dedicated her life to helping, even if he was willing to help her with the grants and such.

She was asking him to church because it was the polite thing to do. Not from any wish to be with him. She knew she could just go on her own as she had the last two Sundays since he'd rolled into her life. But since he always showed up anyway, standing in the back as though he wasn't sure he should make himself at home, she decided it would be okay for them to go together. As friends.

She took a deep breath and rapped her knuckles against the wood.

The door swung open, startling her back a step. Nick stepped out, pulling the door shut behind him. He wore dark pants and a short-sleeve, button-down shirt. The vivid blue of the shirt contrasted nicely with his tan skin and dark hair. Each time she saw him, his appeal was stronger, more compelling, and robbed her of reasonable thoughts. Where was that indifference she'd tried to muster up?

"Good morning, Claire."

She cleared her throat. "Morning. I wanted to ask if you'd like to attend church with me."

He smiled and held up his Bible, the pocket-size one she'd seen that first day. The thing that had solidified her trust. "I was hoping you'd ask."

Pleasure and relief washed through her. Maybe his faith was stronger than he thought. "Great. We can take my car."

"How about we take my bike?"

Excitement flared. He'd brought the bike home a few days ago. It would cause a bit of a scandal if they arrived together on his Harley. The wildness inside her urged her to accept. But what about Gwen? She held up her index finger. "Just a sec."

She hurried to Gwen's door and rapped sharply before opening the door and peering inside. She couldn't help the relief running through her veins to find the room empty.

"She there?"

Claire pulled the door closed and whirled around saying, "No. She must— Oh!" She found herself nose to chest with Nick. He smelled clean and masculine and…she backed up a half step and bumped against the closed door.

"She must what?"

She swallowed. "Be singing today. Gwen occasionally sings with the band at church."

"Ah. She's already up and gone." He grinned. "So what about that ride?"

Excitement battered against her ribs. "That would be great."

"After you." He motioned toward the stairs.

Claire fairly skipped down, feeling giddy with anticipation. When they got outside, she was touched to see two helmets hanging from the handlebars. Nick plucked off the smaller of the two and handed it to her. "I borrowed it from Joe. The mechanic. It's his wife's."

She raised a brow, unexpectedly delighted by his forethought. "You were pretty sure of yourself."

He flashed her a grin that curled her toes. "I'd promised you a ride," he said.

"True enough." She put the helmet on. He helped her with the buckle. The intimacy of the act made her realize the depth of her fascination with him. And it wasn't just a physical attraction.

Not that that wasn't important. He was gorgeous to her in a way few men were—all tall, dark and alluring. But the care he took with her, the tenderness he showed toward her, made her ache. No matter how hard she tried or how fast she worked at building her defenses up against him, the truth was she was starting to care for him.

And that was as terrifying a thing as sleeping in a dark alley on a snowy night.

But as long as Nick didn't know that she cared, then she wasn't really vulnerable to him. He wouldn't be able to use her feelings against her. He wouldn't be able to ply her head with false words of love and then pressure her to prove her love the way Billy had.

A little voice inside her head whispered that Nick wouldn't take advantage of her. He wasn't like that.

But she wasn't going to risk it. She'd keep her feelings tucked away safe where they'd never see the light of day.

Thankful she'd worn her royal-blue capri pants with her brown leather mules, she climbed on the bike behind him and settled herself a hand's length from his back.

She listened to his instructions of where to place her feet and her hands. As he told her to lean with him when he leaned and to sit straight when he sat straight, she decided she didn't want to think about her heart or the risks of caring. She wanted to enjoy this moment, savor the thrill of riding on the back of his Harley.

When the bike came to life beneath her, excitement shuddered through her at the same tempo of the rumbling engine. Nick twisted around to look at her. She nodded and offered him a wide smile, hoping he'd see how much this meant to her.

The twinkle in his eyes said he got the message.

Then they were off, rolling through town, the pace too sedate, but necessary. Claire waved at several people and giggled when they just stared. The ride wasn't nearly long or wild enough for Claire. In a matter of minutes, they pulled into the Community Church's parking lot.

People were filing through the church's open doors. The building was beautiful with its white steeple, black bell tower and, colorful stained-glass windows.

She slid off the bike. Nick took the helmet from her and hooked it on the handlebars.

"Thank you," she said as he turned to offer her his arm.

"Later we'll take a more scenic ride."

Her heart thumped at the prospect.

Inside, they found a seat near the Jordan family. Soon the congregation was singing with the music director. Claire enjoyed listening to Nick's deep voice and noted with pleasure that he knew the songs. The other two times he'd come to the church, he'd been too far away for her to hear him.

When Gwen stepped up to the microphone, Claire smiled with pride for the once rebellious, feisty girl who had turned into a beautiful young woman with a bright future.

The worship service ended and the pastor, a man in his midforties, stepped to the podium. Claire liked Pastor Gary. He was real and humble. His sermons always touched her, as if God were speaking directly to her.

Pastor Gary directed the congregation to Micah 6:8. Claire absorbed the message, sensing God's presence and feeling His grace as Pastor Gary talked of three things God required of His people. To act justly, love mercy and walk humbly with God. God was looking for an ethical response from His people. In Claire's heart, she reaffirmed her vow to remain honest in all she did, to cherish compassionate faithfulness, and to be in submission to God and His word.

When the service ended and the final prayer given, Claire glanced at Nick. His expression was pensive.

"You okay?" she asked.

He blinked and then focused his attention on her. She liked looking into his deep dark eyes, so full of intelligence and compassion.

"I was thinking about The Zone."

"And what were you thinking?"

"To generate community support, you need to generate community awareness. You can do that by getting the community involved."

She cocked her head to the side. "How do I get the community involved?"

"Create a task force of people willing to brainstorm and implement some fund-raising ideas that could involve the community at large."

"How do I create a task force?"

He smiled. "Ask people to help."

Easier said than done. "Like who?"

"Mrs. Wellington, Lori and Peggy Jordan. I'm sure they'd jump at the chance to help out."

And be blessed. She smiled ruefully. "You're right, they would."

"Mrs. Wellington is over there." He pointed in the direction of the large maple where several ladies had gathered to chat.

She bit her lip. Ripples of panic kept her feet planted to the ground. This was going to be hard. How did she ask for help and still be self-sufficient?

"I'll come find you in a bit," he said, giving her a little nudge, forcing her feet forward a step, before moving away through the crowd of churchgoers congregating on the church grounds. She saw several heads turn to watch him as he headed toward the pastor.

Determined not to be distracted by Nick, Claire shifted her gaze away. She wanted to do as he suggested and ask for help for The Zone, but she just didn't know if she had it in her. She liked Nick's idea. And it wasn't like she was asking help for herself. It was for the cause.

Though the rationale helped, she stumbled and sputtered as she approached each lady and told her what she needed.

An hour later, a task force had been assembled, consisting of seven women. Claire was grateful for all the ladies' enthusiasm. They decided to head to the bakery for coffee and pastries while discussing ideas, but first Sandy insisted she and Nick accept their invitation for dinner that night. Promising she'd talk with Nick about that, Claire headed off to find him.

She found Nick deep in conversation with Pastor Gary. The two men stopped talking when she approached.

"Hello, Claire," Pastor Gary said. He was of average height and athletic, with medium brown hair and a sweet demeanor that made him look younger than his midforties.

"Pastor Gary, that was a wonderful message today."

He inclined his head. "I'm glad you thought so. How are things coming with The Zone?"

She slanted a glance at Nick. "They're progressing nicely."

"Good, good. I'll keep you in my prayers. And if the church can do anything, you let me know. We're here for you, Claire."

"Thank you," she said, meaning it.

"If you'll excuse me, I see my wife beckoning." Pastor Gary walked away.

"You ready?" Nick asked, his dark eyes warm like rich coffee.

"Actually, I'm headed to Tessa's Bakery with some of the ladies to discuss The Zone."

Nick's smiled showed his approval. "That's great."

She preened. "I'll catch a ride back with Lori."

"Good enough. Later, then."

"Okay." She started to walk away but then turned back. "The Wellingtons asked if we'd join them for dinner at their house tonight."

Nick's dark brows flickered briefly in surprise. He hesitated.

"It's no big deal if you don't want to. I'll tell them you have other plans," she offered, thinking he was looking for an out. She didn't know why he'd be uncomfortable with the Wellingtons.

He seemed to decide. "Dinner at their house would be fine."

"You sure?"

"Yes."

Her gaze was captured by his dark intense eyes. He radiated a vitality that pulled at her like a magnet. She placed a hand at the base of her throat as she backed up, trying to break the magnetic force spinning her sense.

"Okay then. I'll see you later," she said.

He inclined his head.

She hurried to join the group of ladies waiting on the sidewalk. She glanced back and watched Nick walk to his bike. A part of her wanted to ditch the ladies and go with him. She forced herself to turn away even as the rumbling purr of the bike's engine raced up her spine.

She needed to stay focused on The Zone, not on her feelings for Nick, which would only lead her to disappointment.

Nick opened the throttle and let the bike scream down the empty back roads on the outskirts of Pineridge. The countryside was lush and green. The trees—evergreens, oak and ash—majestic in their beauty. It felt good to have the wind biting at him. To feel the power of his machine beneath him.

His mind raced with thoughts of Claire, of his intense feelings for her. He struggled with how to define them, how to box them up. He enjoyed the time spent with her. He loved the way she rose to a challenge, the way she offered help without judging. She was so sweet and kind. So stubborn and closed-off. Giving and honest, yet so fragile. He wanted to protect her, to cherish her.

But he had no right to such feelings. He'd had someone to cherish and protect once. Yet he'd failed Serena. He didn't want to put himself in a position to fail again. He didn't want to hurt Claire. It was time to move on.

The repairs to The Zone would be done in a matter of days. Claire now had people she knew were willing to help her. He admired that she'd stepped out of her comfort level to ask for help for The Zone. All she needed was a little push and some confidence. He was gratified to think he'd had something to do with her achieving some self-assurance. Maybe that was God's purpose for bringing him here.

Claire would be okay now. The unruly teenagers hadn't been anywhere near The Zone as far as he could tell, but just to be on the cautious side he'd speak with Officer Bob and make sure he kept an eye on her.

Nick squelched the sting of jealousy that thought brought.

A few more days and he'd be ready to leave, to move on. Only now, he'd have not only his grief and anger to contend with, but also the ache of leaving Claire behind.

Claire stood on the doorstep of the Wellingtons with Nick at her side as if they were a couple. She felt nervous little flutters in her belly.

They weren't a couple.

And though they seemed to have fallen into a friendly, comfortable pattern over the last few weeks, she sure didn't want anyone, including herself, getting any far-out ideas that she and Nick were an item.

Nick leaned over her shoulder to ring the doorbell. His warm breath stirred the little hairs exposed at the nape of her neck by her French twist. She shivered.

"Cold?" he asked and dropped an arm around her shoulders. His big, calloused hand smoothed over her arm.

Stunned by the gesture, her pulse jumped. But instead of moving away from him like she knew she should, she leaned into his wide chest. "I'm good," she murmured, her voice sounding strange, breathy.

The door opened. Dave Wellington, looking comfortable in khaki shorts and a Hawaiian-print shirt, smiled his greeting as his gaze swept over them. "Hello, you two. Welcome."

Claire felt heat rising up her neck past the collar of her white, peasant-style blouse. She broke away from Nick and stepped into the house that was as familiar to her as her aunt's had been.

Nick followed her in and shook hands with Dave.

The hardwood floors of the entryway gleamed beneath a colorful Persian runner. Claire dropped her purse onto an oak side table beneath a gilded mirror. She glanced at her reflection and noticed her flushed complexion. She hoped no one else noticed, especially Nick. She didn't want him to know how he affected her.

Sandy appeared around the corner at the end of the hall. "Come on in to the dining room. Dinner's just about ready." She disappeared back around the corner.

"I'll go see if I can help," Claire said with a quick glance at Nick. He nodded his encouragement.

She walked away as the two men began to talk of sports and such.

We are not a couple, she told herself firmly.

"What can I do to help, Sandy?" Claire asked as she entered the well-appointed kitchen.

Granite tile countertops and dark wood cabinets lined the walls. Sandy pulled out a covered dish from the oven. The aromas of garlic and paprika wafted in the air.

Sandy pointed with one oven-mitted hand toward a large cherry wood hutch. "Would you mind grabbing a trivet and put it on the dining table?"

"Sure." Claire went to the hutch. She noticed a small gold-framed picture on the top shelf, and reached out to touch the images. In the photo, Sandy and Aunt Denise stood with their arms around one another, smiles on their faces.

Claire traced her finger over Aunt Denise's face. Her white-blonde hair shimmered in the June sun. Claire had taken the picture with the camera her aunt had given her for graduation. "I miss you," she whispered.

"I miss her, too, you know," Sandy said quietly from behind Claire.

Blinking back her grief, Claire plucked a square-shaped trivet from the top of a stack and moved to the table. She set it down. "She'd appreciate all you've done for me."

Sandy's brow flickered. "I wish you'd let me do more."

"You do plenty," Claire reassured her. "Should I call in the men?"

Sandy's gaze searched her face. "You like him."

Claire ducked her head. "Should I fill the water glasses?"

Sandy tsked. "You know, it's okay to have feelings for people, Claire. For you to have feelings for Nick. He seems like a good guy. Dave has only good things to say about him. I know Denise would have approved."

Claire knew the older woman meant well. "He'll be leaving soon, Sandy. I can't…I don't want to…" *get hurt*. She waved her hand. "It just wouldn't work." *We are not a couple.*

But later, after they'd eaten and sat on the back porch for coffee and dessert, Claire had the weirdest longing she'd ever experienced.

As she sat next to Nick, their chairs close enough that his jean-clad knee pressed against hers, she wondered what it would be like to be married. To have someone in her life who knew her so well.

She watched the way Sandy and Dave communicated verbally with terms of endearments and little inside phrases that indicated a level of intimacy Claire had never known. She watched the way their affection for one another showed in the little gestures. A hand being held. Sandy offering Dave a bite of her pie, since he'd declared he was dieting. The way they looked at each other with love and life.

She'd been around the Wellingtons since she was

fifteen, but she'd never noticed them as a couple. Until now.

Her attention moved to Nick and she watched him with rapt fascination. He was so at ease, so personable. He kept the conversation going with talk of world events, sports and politics.

And what endeared her to him most was the way he kept her included. Asked her opinion as if really interested in the answer.

When the night wore down and they were leaving, it seemed natural for her to slip her hand into his as they walked back to the car after much hugging by Sandy and Dave.

It wasn't until they were at The Zone that she remembered to remind herself that they weren't a couple—could never be a couple. Couples expected things from each other, needed each other to complete the unit. Couplehood was not for her.

She whispered a quick good-night and fled to her room.

Light seeped out from beneath the edge of Nick's door. He wasn't asleep. Claire breathed a sigh of relief that was short-lived as a wave of panic hit her. She'd spent the last twenty minutes trying to banish her thoughts about Nick and couples and marriage.

She'd settled on a plan of action. Help Nick mend the rift with his parents and fulfill the purpose God had for bringing him into her life. Once that was accomplished, she could send him on his way and she'd go back to being self-sufficient and alone without him.

She frowned as that last thought brought a twinge of pain. That was what she wanted, wasn't it?

Mentally shaking away that thread of thinking, she said a quick prayer, asking for support. She knocked on the door.

"Come in," Nick called.

She opened the door. He sat on the bed with his broad back propped against the wall. He wore a white cotton T-shirt and light gray drawstring shorts. Dark hair covered his athletic legs stretched out in front of him.

She sucked in a quick breath.

He looked good, comfortable and appealing. And Claire realized she'd probably made a big mistake by not waiting until morning.

She swallowed and tried to find her voice. "I brought you something."

He raised his brows and set aside the book he was reading. A Bible. Her heart smiled at the knowledge that even in his pain, Nick still sought the Lord.

He swung his legs to the side and stood. She moved forward and held out the pack of stationery—plain cream paper with gold edging that her aunt had once given to her.

His gaze flicked to the stationery, then to her face.

She offered him a smile. "I was thinking you might want to write to your parents. Let them know you're all right. They could even write back to you here."

A thoughtful expression crossed his face, though she could see a shadow lurking in the dark depths of his eyes.

"I think it might help you," she ventured, wishing he'd say something.

"You're all about helping people, aren't you," he said dryly.

She blinked, unsure whether he was making fun of her or not. "I like to help."

"Makes you feel good," he stated.

She drew in her chin. "Yes, I guess so. I never really thought about that."

A slow smile formed on his well-shaped mouth. "You have a good heart, Claire."

Warmed by his words, she smiled back. He reached out to take the stationery packet and their fingers connected. She released her hold. The last thing she needed was more fuel for her unwanted attraction.

"Thank you, Claire."

She squirmed slightly under his knowing gaze, but was thankful he'd accepted her attempt to help. She only hoped he'd use the stationery and write to his parents. "You're welcome."

He cocked one eyebrow. "Was there something else?"

"Uh, no."

His mouth quirked up as if he knew exactly the effect he had on her.

She backed up. "See you in the morning."

She left, shutting the door firmly behind her. With his tempting-as-chocolate grin imprinted on her brain, she undoubtedly would have another restless night's sleep.

Chapter Nine

Three days later, Claire listened and didn't hear the noise of construction that had greeted her every morning for the past few weeks. A bird chirped outside her window as if he sensed her good humor. She stretched, then threw off the covers and quickly dressed.

Last night after dark Nick had announced that the work was done and she'd have her kitchen fully back today.

With a light step, she hurried from her room to view the repaired wall, new back porch and door. From the inside she couldn't even tell there'd been a fire. She rushed out the new back door and down the steps with Little Nick nipping at her heels.

Standing in the middle of the backyard, she looked at the gray building. It looked great. Gone were the saws and piles of wood, both old and new. Nick had even swept the walkway of the sawdust debris.

Her heart swelled with gratitude for all he'd done. He'd worked so hard to finish the job and keep the cost under what the insurance would pay. She was also thankful he'd given her the push she needed to ask for help. The committee had agreed on a picnic-basket auction as The Zone's first fund-raiser.

Nick had made her see how much others wanted to be asked and how much people were willing to give.

She glanced up at the cloud-dotted sky. "Thank you for bringing Nick into my life."

Now she needed to thank Nick and let him know what a blessing he'd been. Not that she was attached to him or anything. Just grateful he'd roared into her life when he had. A little bubble of sadness escaped, reminding her that he would eventually leave. She'd deal with his departure when she had to. Not today. Today was too beautiful.

She looked around for the puppy and spotted him digging under the lilac bush.

"No digging," she admonished with a wag of her finger. He ran over and pawed at her shins. She bent down and scratched his head, thankful no one had claimed him.

Little Nick followed closely at her heels as she went back inside. She put him in his crate and walked up the stairs to Nick's door. She knocked lightly.

"Come in."

She opened the door and froze as he straightened from zipping his saddlebag closed. He was wearing his black leather motorcycle riding clothes. He looked like he had the day they first met. Had that only been a month ago?

"What are you doing?" Her stomach rolled with the implications of his actions, his clothes.

He shrugged. "Time to move on."

A shivery, panicky feeling grabbed her, squeezing tight. "You didn't say anything about leaving last night."

He threw her an odd look. "The repairs are done, Claire."

"Yes, but…" Her heart raced in her ears. "You're not staying for the auction?"

His dark brows rose. "That's two weeks away." He picked up his bag. "There's no reason for me to stay, is there?"

A reason for him to stay? Her mind worked frantically, looking for something to hold on to, a plausible reason to ask him to stay because she wasn't ready for this to happen. She hadn't had a chance to deal with it. She hadn't helped him with his parents. "Sandy and Dave will want to say goodbye. Everyone will want to say goodbye. You can't just up and leave. That's not fair."

He moved toward her. The scent of man and leather swirled around her, tantalizing in the depth of emotion and memory the scent evoked. A sense of safety remembered, cherished. His arms around her, carrying her out of harm's way. His kindness, his honor.

"And you, Claire? Do you want to say goodbye?" He ran a knuckle down her cheek.

"Yes. No. I mean, I want…" Her lungs contracted, trapping her in-drawn breath. The world spun, sending her off balance, out of control. She hated this feeling. Hated the need welling up, threatening to drown her.

She wanted him to stay. She wanted him to *want* to stay. And she'd willingly beg for his attention.

The air left her chest in a rush like the tie on a balloon coming undone. She'd promised herself she'd never go to this place again. This vulnerable, needy state.

She'd feared he'd use her feelings against her. But she was using them against herself. Disappointment and anger clogged her throat. Filled her soul.

She stepped back, away from the protective shelter of his presence, away from the feelings crushing her heart.

She had to put an end to this. To whatever it was between them. She swallowed the bitter pill of her own expectations and forced a smile. "I wanted to thank you for all your hard work. It was a blessing you came when you did." She strove for an indifference she didn't feel. "You can leave when you want."

Forcing her legs to move at a sedate pace, she went down the stairs, uncrated Little Nick and led him outside to the park across the street. She followed as he raced ahead through the grass. She was on the far side of the park when she heard the growl of Nick's Harley. She didn't look back nor did she wipe at the tears streaming down her face.

Nick cruised down Main Street without really seeing Pineridge. He'd seen the hurt darken Claire's blue eyes. Had heard the reedy tenor of her voice that betrayed her feelings.

He wanted to apologize for letting their relationship ever seem more than it was. He'd tried to keep his distance. Tried to stay unemotional and detached, but that had proved impossible. There was so much about Claire to like. To care about.

And the other night at the Wellingtons, he'd become painfully aware how thoroughly she'd melted the ice around his heart.

He'd imagined a future with her. As he'd observed the love between Sandy and Dave, he'd ached to have a spouse to share his life with, to grow old with. And that scared him. He didn't want to risk the pain and the grief of loss again.

So it was time to leave.

But Claire was right about one thing. He shouldn't leave without properly saying goodbye to the people of Pineridge. The community had embraced him, accepted him and made him feel again. A lot of that had to do with Claire. She'd set the tone. He pulled off to the side of the street and parked, but didn't move.

Beneath his breath, he muttered, "Lord, I don't understand what You want of me. I live my life the way I think I should according to Your word and then You let it all crash down around me. So I try again to seek You and I land here. But to what end? For more pain? To hurt Claire?" He shook his head. "I don't get it. When will You give me peace? That's all I'm asking for, Lord. Some peace."

"Hey, Andrews," a masculine voice called.

Nick twisted around on the seat toward the sidewalk. Officer Bob walked toward him, his clothes pressed and his badge shining. Nick removed his helmet and hung it on the handlebars. "Officer," he acknowledged.

"Went by The Zone this morning. Good work."

Nick hid a smile at the grudging tone of Bob's praise. "I had help."

"So I've heard."

Nick raised a questioning brow at him.

Bob seemed flustered. "You know how people talk. You and Claire have been a hot topic."

Nick shot him a sharp glance. Bob held up a hand. "Hey, everyone loves Claire. No one wants to see her get hurt."

"Good. Then you'll keep an eye on her?"

Bob's gaze narrowed. "You leaving town?"

Nick nodded. "After a few goodbyes."

He considered Nick for a moment then conceded. "Sure, I'll keep an eye on her." His expression turned rueful. "If she'll let me."

Nick almost felt bad for the guy. He knew Claire wasn't interested in the young officer. At least not in a romantic way.

"Don't let me keep you from your job, Officer." Nick stuck out his hand. After the slightest hesitation, Bob accepted Nick's handshake.

"You know where you're headed?" Bob asked, his tone a bit more congenial.

He shrugged. "North, maybe."

"Well, good luck." Bob gave a curt nod and then ambled away, leaving Nick with an unnerving twinge of possessiveness toward Claire.

Rationally, Nick knew the other man would do his best to protect Claire, but would he make her smile, make her laugh? Would anyone be able to breach the walls she'd constructed to keep everyone at arm's length? Walls Nick had tried to scale and at times thought he'd conquered. But now he had to leave Claire with her barricaded life. He had to keep moving.

Nick headed into Tessa's bakery to start the goodbyes. Something he'd never felt the need for in the last two years until he'd met a blue-eyed blonde named Claire.

Nick waved one last time to Sandy and Dave Wellington as he left their modest two-story home in a residential neighborhood on the east side of town. He liked the older couple and was thankful Claire had such caring people in her life. But seeing them made him realize he couldn't leave things the way they were between him and Claire.

He'd hurt her. Plain and simple. Her indifference wasn't real. It was her defense. Against him. Guilt stabbed at him. She did care for him. As a friend, at least. He hoped it wasn't more, because there couldn't be more.

He headed back toward town, back toward The Zone. He owed her an apology and a proper goodbye.

As he turned the corner and The Zone came into view, his gaze zeroed in on the slashes of red marring the side of the building. Anger and worry burned in his gut. Bringing the bike to a halt, he noticed Claire sitting under the tree, her knees drawn up and her head resting on her folded arms.

She looked up at him as he approached. His heart

wrenched at the sight of her red-rimmed eyes and tear-stained cheeks. He rushed to her side and hunkered down. "Are you all right?"

She blinked. "What are you doing here?"

He captured a tear with the pad of his finger. "I came back to apologize and to say goodbye."

Her dark blonde brows drew together. She pulled away from his touch. "You don't owe me an apology."

Her withdrawal stung. He needed to make it right. "I do. I shouldn't have let you think my staying was more—"

She cut him off with a raised hand. "Don't even go there. You did what you said you were going to do. Now, say your goodbye and ride away." She flicked her hand at him.

His jaw tightened with frustration. She didn't give an inch. "I'm not going anywhere."

She jumped to her feet, her blue eyes blazing. "Excuse me? What's that supposed to mean?"

He slowly rose. His temper hung by a thread. *"Hello."* He gestured to the wall. "Those punks came back. You think I'm going to leave you while they're still out there running loose?"

"Oh, yeah, I'm terrified of red spray paint. Please." She placed her hands on her hips. "I don't need a hero. I don't need you. I can take care of this myself."

He ignored the unexpected hurt her words caused. He clenched his fists. "You *should* be terrified, Claire. And thankful it was only spray paint and not some deadly stunt like the last time. You don't know that next time they won't come back with a gun."

Terror stormed through his veins.

God had sent him here for a reason, all right. To stop those kids and somehow he'd lost sight of that. He wasn't going to let anything happen to Claire. He stalked away, heading for his bike.

"What are you doing?" she called after him.

Grabbing his helmet, he sat and turned to stare at her. She looked like an angel from one of her drawings. Sunlight flittered through the tree branches, kissing her strawberry-blond hair with shimmering gold. Her blue eyes captivated him. Drew him in and made him aware that he was failing miserably at staying emotionally detached.

"I'm going to teach those punks a lesson they won't forget."

God was giving him another chance to protect the woman in his life. No matter how tenuous that position. He wasn't going to blow it a second time.

Claire's insides clenched with dread. "Wait!"

She ran after Nick's bike as he roared away, but stopped abruptly. There was no chance she'd catch him. Thank goodness he didn't even know where to look. Did he?

She ran back to The Zone, grabbed her keys and jumped in her little car. Too late to follow him, but she could head him off, if he did know where the kids hung out.

She didn't understand his rage, or the vengeance so obvious in his attitude. She'd seen it that first day and now it was back.

She pressed the gas pedal, pushing the car as fast as she dared.

She couldn't let him go half-cocked into a situation where someone could get hurt. Where *he* could get hurt.

"Please, God, don't let anything bad happen."

Anger, thick and hot like lava, boiled in Nick's blood. He drove to where he'd seen the blond kid. The industrial park. They had to be somewhere. Why not here? The warehouses were less visible with more hiding spots.

Nick drove slowly past the empty buildings. Another warehouse set back farther from the paved road on a gravel drive caught his attention.

Wooden planks boarded the windows. A chain lock looped around the handle of the door. Across the front of the building were the words "Pineridge Storage Company" in faded green lettering. A desolate feeling squeezed in on the anger burning in his gut. This seemed a likely spot.

Leaving his bike in the shade of a tree, he walked around the building looking for an opening. He found a hole in the wall on the side of the structure. The scuffs in the dirt and the smudges of handprints on the wall made him think this opening was well-used. He bent down and peered in, but saw only blackness.

Tires crunching on the gravel drew his attention. He peered around the corner. Claire's green Subaru pulled to a stop and the driver's door flung open. She stepped out.

He shook his head, exasperation tightened his jaw. He shouldn't be surprised to see her. She'd probably known all along where the teens hid out. Serena had been just as headstrong. His heart contracted painfully in his chest.

He forced away the grief and concentrated on Claire.

She spotted him. Her mouth pressed into a firm line and with purposeful strides she moved toward the building, toward him. He met her before she could see the opening.

"Claire, you shouldn't be here."

"No one should be here," she stated abruptly.

He took her by the elbow and steered her back toward her car. "You need to leave."

She jerked out of his grasp. "Don't think you can manhandle me because you're bigger and stronger."

He drew back in surprise. "I would never physically hurt you, Claire."

The sparks of anger receded in her eyes and she took a deep breath, letting the air out in a steady stream. "I overreacted. I know you wouldn't intentionally hurt me."

But he had hurt her. Unintentionally.

He fought the urge to wrap her in his arms and shield her from the world. He was in deep enough as it was. "Maybe all this business with the teens is finally catching up to you."

"Maybe." She looked to the building. "What do you intend to do if you find them?"

He ran a hand through his hair. "I don't know. Scare some sense into them, I guess."

She turned her gaze back on him. The pain in her eyes clawed at him with searing intensity. He had no shield to protect himself from her. "Most of these kids have suffered from abuse, neglect, starvation. You honestly think bullying tactics will work?"

He set his jaw against the plummeting sensation of getting sucked into her pain, which threatened to undercut his anger. "I have to do something, Claire."

"Why? What personal vendetta are you trying to carry out here?"

Her pointed question blasted a hole right through his heart with satellite-guided accuracy. He clenched his back teeth. "Someone has to protect you."

"This isn't really about me, though, is it?"

Guilt wrapped greedy fingers around his lungs, forcing the air out and refusing to allow any in. He spun away.

He couldn't do anything about the past, he was realizing that now. But he could do something about the future. Claire's future—and her safety. He'd do whatever it took to make it clear she wasn't to be messed with.

Even stay?

No! That wasn't a possibility. There was too much at stake—his heart, Claire's life. The vortex of pain endangered them all.

He couldn't stay, but he could make sure these kids didn't bother her again.

He stalked back to the hole in the building with Claire dogging his heels. "Stay out here."

Her expression told him clearly what she thought about that.

He bent down and slipped through the opening. He waited a moment as his eyes adjusted to the dim-

ness. The room had high ceilings and bare walls
with exposed beams and the concrete floor was lit-
tered with debris and dirt. The smell of neglect
clogged his throat.

Claire followed him through the opening. "I don't
think anyone's here," she whispered. "Let's go."

She was still trying to keep him away from the
teens.

He pointed to a big sliding door on one wall. At
his back, Claire grabbed a fistful of his shirt. Nick
picked his way through the rubble of broken
Sheetrock, wood and metal to stand by the door.
Several footprints tracked in the dirt in front of the
door.

Bracing himself, with Claire still behind him, he
slowly slid the door open.

An inner signal cautioned him to tread with care.
He stepped back and over a few steps so he had a better view of the inner room. Claire stepped in tandem
with him, staying behind him, allowing him to shield
her.

A horrific thought crept into his brain. What if
they did have gun? The possibility was within the
realm of his experience with teenagers. They didn't
respect life—theirs or anyone else's.

A shadow crossed his peripheral vision. A second
later something launched at him. Claire's scream
echoed inside his head. A shoulder rammed into his
solar plexus. He absorbed the impact, compartmen-
talizing the pain. He wrapped his arms around the
body and squeezed, lifting the smaller person off the
ground.

A toe connected with his shin. He gritted his teeth and squeezed harder. "Knock it off!" he roared to the squirming boy in his arms.

"Let go!"

Nick did, loosening his hold, and the boy fell to the ground with a thump. The boy, Tyler, scrambled to the far corner where Mindy and the blond boy stood wide-eyed and visibly trembling.

Claire touched Nick's back. "You okay?"

"Yes." As he stared at the teens, took in their lean faces, the filth, the condition of the place, his stomach rolled. This was no place for teenagers to be living, but that's exactly what it was to them—home. The makeshift cardboard beds, the empty take-out cartons piled in one corner. So that's what Claire had done with their leftover pizza and Chinese food.

On the floor by one of the beds, a soup can held a handful of wildflowers. Pity rose, sharp and choking. Nick's gaze snagged on a partially hidden spray can with red smudges.

He squared his shoulders and trampled down any softening. "We need to talk."

Tyler stood and faced him. "We have nothing to say to you."

Nick begrudgingly admired the kid's courage. "Too bad, because I do. Let's get something straight. I don't want to hear any lies or excuses. I know you vandalized The Zone today. And I'm pretty sure you set the fire." One look at Mindy's guilt-ridden face confirmed his suspicion.

"You can't prove anything," Tyler countered.

"We'll see what the police think."

That was the only course of action to take. Claire was right. No matter how much he'd like to threaten the teens or make them pay, he couldn't. They'd suffered far worse than he could ever hope to dish out. But the authorities could do something. Get them help. Keep them away from Claire.

"You can't turn them in."

His gut clenched. He stared at Claire in disbelief. "Not this again."

"You don't understand." Unshed tears glistened in her eyes.

That vortex of pain had a powerful draw. "Then make me understand."

"The authorities can only do so much. They'll be sent to juvenile detention and then back to their homes or to foster homes. They'll only run away again."

"That's right," Tyler interjected. "I'm not going back there."

Nick frowned. "That's not my problem."

She clutched his arm. "It's everyone's problem. Especially if you're a believer."

He shook his head as more bottled-up rage spurted through him. So many times his parents had pushed for him to let go of his anger and forgive that kid, claiming God would want him to. They'd pushed and pushed until he couldn't take it and he'd left. "Don't even try to lay that guilt trip on me."

She gave him a pained expression. "It's not about guilt. It's about doing what's right even if it's uncomfortable. About showing compassion, even when it's undeserved."

She cut the air with her hand. "No. Especially when it's undeserved. It's about loving the unlovable. Jesus calls us to love as He did."

A desperate plea for understanding shone bright in her eyes. "I've been where these kids are. I've lived this."

His mind reeled from her words. It wasn't possible. Not Claire. Not sweet, nurturing, soft-hearted Claire.

"What do you mean you've lived this?" He stared at her in shock, trying to reconcile her words with what he knew of Claire. No. This couldn't be true.

Chapter Ten

She waved away his question. "These kids aren't criminals." The conviction in her voice set Nick's teeth on edge.

Whoa! Back up. He wanted to know about her. All the time they'd spent together, discussed The Zone and the work she wanted to accomplish, and she'd kept hidden an important piece of information.

He forced himself to concentrate on the issue at hand. "You don't think destroying property and putting your life in danger isn't criminal?"

"If I believed turning them in would change anything for them, I'd do it."

A knot of wrath lodged itself in his chest. "It isn't for them, it's for you. Your safety. Shouldn't they pay the consequences for their actions?"

Like the punk who'd killed Serena. That kid should rot for eternity in jail, but because of the kid's age he'd be set free one day.

"Yes, of course. It's just…"

His hands clenched at his sides. "Coddling them isn't the answer, Claire."

She straightened. "Not coddle. Guide, mentor. Lead them down the right path."

"You're too idealistic for your own good." He made a sweeping gesture toward where the teens stood and stared at them. "Kids like these just want to destroy."

Her expression turned scornful. "You are so clueless. You have no idea what it's like to be alone and scared. Desperate. Digging through the trash to eat. To have everyone treat you like scum. To have the people who should protect you just as soon beat you or...or worse."

He flinched. Had the "worse" been done to her? His stomach churned, but he resisted allowing her to diminish his anger with her dramatic words.

"And you want to send them to juvie." As she pointed a finger at him, tight lines formed around her mouth. "I don't mean to be disrespectful of the system, but you want to put kids who still might have a chance in with harder, meaner kids. What do you think they're going to learn?"

She raised a mocking brow. "Huh? I'll tell you. They're going to learn to be harder and meaner and come out angrier. Then you're talking about the kids who use guns, the kids who grow into criminal adults. The prisons are full of them."

Anger and grief surfaced, taunting him as he stared into Claire's shimmering eyes. He rejected her words. Wouldn't let her bleeding heart affect him.

Lord, what am I suppose to do now?

He ran a hand through his hair. Unbelievable. She had been one of *them*. One of the kind who'd robbed him of his love. His life.

What was he doing here? He should be miles away by now, not facing off with a blue-eyed blonde over some runaways.

He leveled a hard look on the teens. "This is the way it's going down. You want a get-out-of-jail-free card? You be at The Zone in one hour. The three of you are going to clean up the mess you made. I'll find jobs for you to do to work off the debt you owe Claire. And no drugs. If there's even the slightest hint that you're using or have brought drugs with you, you go to jail."

"Hey, I'm not…" Tyler began, but stopped short as Nick took a step forward.

Mindy put a hand on Tyler's arm, much the way Claire had done to Nick that day in the park. Tyler turned toward her, and she shook her head, exerting some unseen female power.

"Thank you, Nick."

Claire's softly spoken words drew his attention away from the teens and deepened his frown. The gratefulness, the admiration in her voice, ripped a hole in his heart. He held up a hand. "Don't."

He didn't want either of those things from her. He wanted nothing from her. Pressure built in his chest. Only her safety. "Leave with me now, Claire, and let them make their choice."

He couldn't keep the edge out of his voice or his words from being a challenge. A demand. A plea.

She stared at his hand and then turned her gaze to the teens. They stared at her mutely.

After a tense moment, she straightened. Lifting her chin, she narrowed her eyes at the three kids. "Trust me—come to The Zone. I know what you're going through. I've been there. I can help. Please, come."

She placed her hand in Nick's. The pressure holding tight to his chest eased and tenderness filled him. He squeezed her hand and led her out of the building.

Claire dropped his hand and wrapped her arms around his waist.

"Hey, what's this?" He placed his hands on her shoulders.

She beamed up at him. "Just because."

Looking down into her smiling face, feeling her slender arms hugging him, he felt a jolt of emotion he couldn't identify. Then slowly, calmness seeped in, taking the edge off his anger. He rubbed her shoulders as he tried to come to grips with the caring that invaded his heart. "I hope you won't be too crushed if they don't show up."

Her smile turned rueful, determined. "They'll show up even if I have to drag them there myself."

He frowned. "Claire!"

Her expression became playful. "Kidding."

She gave him a quick squeeze then moved away from him and started walking toward her car. He followed, wishing he could believe her. Claire was a fixer, a caretaker.

A runaway.

His gut clenched. He pushed the horror aside. She wasn't like the others, the troublemakers. The killers. She'd turned her life around.

But how many lives had she ruined in the process?

* * *

Claire picked up the ball Little Nick had dropped at her feet, then tossed it away. The puppy's short legs scrambled as he chased the ball across The Zone's small yard.

She was aware of Nick's intense gaze, could feel his unspoken questions. She couldn't believe she'd blurted out that she'd been a runaway.

The look on his face had cut her like the pointed end of a switchblade. The way she'd known it would.

He wouldn't—couldn't—understand. He'd had a home. A loving family. She'd only been able to dream about those things and vow to offer that kind of care and concern to other runaways.

She glanced at her wristwatch. Only twenty minutes left for the teens to show up. Anxiety twisted inside of her.

If they didn't show, Nick would go to the police. So far he'd displayed compassion and mercy by not contacting the authorities, but she doubted he'd see it that way. He was so intent on judging and condemning all runaways. All teens.

Why?

If she had an ounce of wisdom in her, she'd give up trying to solve the puzzle of Nick. But she didn't know if she could do that.

As she wandered to the edge of the walkway and stared off in the distance toward the road that led to the warehouse, doubts filtered in. The kids weren't ready to trust them. They needed more time, more guidance, to help them realize they could make good choices.

She spun on her heel and nearly tripped over Little Nick. He dropped the ball from his mouth. She kicked it and paced back to the stairs where Nick sat, his pose casual, unconcerned. She briefly met his gaze, his eyes inky and observant, before turning and walking the short distance down the walkway again.

She glanced at her watch. Fifteen more minutes. Where were they? A bird flew across the cloudless sky, a black streak that disappeared behind the towering evergreens of the park. If the kids didn't show by ten after, she was going to go get them.

"Claire."

"Hmm?"

"Come sit down. Your pacing isn't going to make them come any faster."

She acknowledged the truth in his words with a ruefully toss of her head. "I'm too antsy to sit."

"You can't control this, Claire. They're going to do whatever they're going to do."

She narrowed her gaze, chafing against his words because she knew he was right. "You hope they don't show. Then you can turn them in."

A muscle tightened in his jaw. He wasn't so unconcerned. "It doesn't matter what I hope."

"They're just kids. I should have stayed. They need me to help them."

He raised a brow. "Maybe they need the opportunity to earn your trust."

Where did he get off sounding so confident and sure of what the teenagers needed? He didn't have a degree in psychology, hadn't been through the

Young Life training. Had never lived the lives of these kids. He didn't even like them.

Yet, something inside her wanted to let him be the one to bear the burden, to be the one to take responsibility. The temptation to let him rose and she hated the weakness in herself. She would not need him.

She took a deep breath, concentrating on his words about control and the simple truth that somehow she'd let it slip away. She wasn't in control and neither was Nick.

All she could do was pray the kids would show up on their own. That God would speak to their hearts.

It was hard to wait. Hard to release the worry and anxiety.

She wanted to ask Nick why he hated the teens so much, but she knew that if she did he'd ask about her past, about being a runaway. A dicey subject at best. One better left alone.

The puppy pawed at her shins, the ball forgotten. She sat on the step next to Nick and stroked Little Nick's yellow coat as he lay down beside her. She resisted the urge to check her watch again.

Then Nick's hand on her knee sent her thoughts scattering. Her gaze lifted. His attention zeroed in on three people walking down the road toward them. Her heart leapt with relief. God had answered her prayers. The kids were coming.

"I knew they'd come," she boasted.

One corner of his full mouth twisted upward in a mocking grin. "Didn't you just."

Heat stole up her neck and settled in her cheeks.

She lifted her chin. "Okay, maybe I doubted it. A little."

He laughed. The dry, brittle sound scraped along her nerves. The first battle had been won, but the war to save the teens had just started.

Would Nick be an ally or an enemy?

"So, we're here," Tyler said with a large dose of insolence lacing his words as he and the other two teens stopped in front of The Zone.

Nick struggled with the desire to grab Tyler by the scruff of the neck and shake him. Instead, he flexed his fingers and leveled a stern glare on the three teens. He decided against commenting on their timing. "Follow me."

He led them to where he'd set up the leftover paint and clean brushes near the side of the house. He pointed toward the supplies. "There you go. Get started."

Defiance lit up Tyler's eyes, but the other two headed over without hesitation. Nick raised a brow. Tyler shrugged and turned away to join the other two. Nick let out a heavy breath, thankful the situation hadn't turned into another stand-off with the kid.

Claire stepped up beside him. "We can't let them go back to that warehouse."

A burst of anger tightened his gut. His gaze slid to her. The light of battle shone bright in her eyes. "And what do you suggest we do with them?"

She blinked up at him as if he should already know the answer to that question—which he had a sinking feeling he did.

"They'll stay here. Won't take me but a few minutes to make the beds in the two rooms, clear away a few boxes."

He grimaced, his mind rebelling against sleeping with the enemy underfoot. "I had a feeling you were going to say that."

"What would you have me do, Nick? They've come this far, trusted this much. I can't send them back out there."

The dusty warehouse with the makeshift beds and that pitiful tin can full of flowers flashed in his mind. "Yeah, I know."

She gave him a smug, sidelong glance. "You're a good man, Nick Andrews."

He snorted. He was insane to be getting so mixed up and entangled with them all. Now how was he going to leave Claire and Pineridge when the teens would be sleeping at The Zone?

That evening, Claire prepared a simple meal. Baked chicken with potatoes and carrots. A sprinkle of dill over the top. Nothing fancy, but one of her favorite recipes from Aunt Denise.

"Can I do anything?" Mindy asked. She stood at the threshold of the kitchen, uncertainty written across her face.

Claire appreciated her manners. She understood the girl's uncertainty, could still remember how she'd felt when she'd first come to live with Aunt Denise. The same way Gwen had been when she'd first come to live with Claire and her aunt. Unsure of her role, wanting to belong but afraid to hope she would.

Mindy was opening a door, hoping to be admitted. The girl wanted to be helpful, be a part of something. Claire understood that deep down they all wanted to belong. "Would you set the table? The plates are in the cupboard by the fridge and glasses are above the sink."

Claire walked to the edge of the living room and called to the boys lounging on the floor. "Johnny, Tyler."

Tyler ignored her.

Johnny jumped up. "Yes?"

"Wash up for dinner, please. Restroom's over there." She pointed to the open door under the stairs.

Knowing it was best to assert her authority from the get-go, Claire wiped her hands on a dishtowel and strode all the way into the living room. She stopped in front of the TV. To her astonishment, Little Nick was stretched out on his back and Tyler's hand was gently stroking the puppy's soft underbelly.

The urge to snatch the puppy away gripped her with a fierce hold, but she forced it down. She wanted Tyler to feel trusted so he'd learn to trust her.

"Tyler. The polite thing to do when someone talks to you is to acknowledge them."

He stared at her knees. "What?"

"Are you hungry?" she asked, patiently.

He lifted a shoulder in a careless shrug.

"Well, I can't force you to eat. If you would like to join us, please wash up in the bathroom and then come to the table."

She stared at the teen. The hard lines in his face

belonged on an adult, not a fifteen-year-old kid. His clothes were filthy. She'd have to do something about that.

When she'd been arranging the rooms upstairs, she'd found a box of clothes Sandy had given her that had once belonged to her twins. There had to be some jeans and T-shirts in the boxes that would fit the teenagers. Maybe decent clothes would help Tyler feel more civilized.

The back door opened. Nick walked in, bringing with him a high level of energy that buzzed in the air and made Claire shiver with awareness. He wore black twill pants that hugged his body attractively, and a black T-shirt. He looked as dark and dangerous as a caged panther she'd once seen at the zoo.

Tyler shifted in the beanbag chair. His gaze darted to Nick and then to the front door. Claire had the distinct impression that if she weren't in his path, Tyler would make a break for the door.

Standing her ground, Claire smiled at Nick. "I hope you're hungry. We're just about to eat."

Nick glanced at Mindy and then Tyler. "I'm not hungry."

Johnny stepped out of the bathroom and froze. Claire frowned. All this tension made for a really bad beginning. She touched Tyler's arm. He flinched away as if he expected her to cuff him upside the head. Claire's heart twisted. "The bathroom's free. Why don't you go wash up?"

He scowled with his chin jutting out and marched past her to the restroom. He closed the door with a snap.

She ushered Johnny into the kitchen. "Why don't you help Mindy with the glasses? There's juice and milk in the fridge." To Nick she said, "You can wash up at the sink. If you prefer not to sit at the table, fill your plate and eat where you'd like."

His dark brows drew together. "Claire, I—"

"It's okay." She understood that he didn't feel the same about the teens as she did. She understood that this was a hard transition for them all. What she didn't understand was Nick's continued anger.

Nick filled his plate and then headed out the back door. Claire felt a stab of sadness and disappointment but she quickly smoothed over the little wound in her heart. She couldn't expect anything from Nick. He wasn't going to be a permanent fixture in her life. She should just be thankful he hadn't turned the kids in.

Claire wished Gwen hadn't had to work tonight. Claire could have used an ally.

Dinner with the three teens was silent and fast. By the way the kids slammed their food down, she figured it had been a long while since they'd had a decent meal. Satisfaction surged through her. She was making a difference in their lives. Just as she had in Gwen's.

As they were finishing the meal, Nick returned. He rinsed his plate and sat on the stool at the counter off to Claire's left, perched like a huge eagle waiting for its prey.

Claire explained the house rules to the kids. No swearing, no drugs. On Sundays everyone attends church. Each person would be expected to clear their own plate, make their bed and pile their laundry by the door. "When we're done eating you can each pick through the boxes of clothes I have upstairs. And find something to wear while I wash what you have on."

Johnny and Mindy finished and without a fuss picked up their plates, carrying them to the sink. Tyler started to leave the table without his plate. Nick cleared his throat, prompting Tyler to glower at him as he picked up his plate. Claire was thankful for Nick's support, only she wished he'd be less threatening about it.

Upstairs, she showed the teens the boxes of clothes. They dug through them with enthusiasm.

Claire gave out towels and washcloths from the bathroom cupboard. "Mindy, why don't you shower first and then the boys can take turns."

"Do you have shampoo?" Mindy asked eagerly.

Claire laughed. "Yes. And conditioner."

"Yay!" Mindy took the clothes she'd decided on and hurried to shower.

Soon all the kids were showered and dressed. Claire carried down their dirty clothes in a basket. In the laundry room, she started the tub filling with water and then pulled a pair of jeans from the basket. She hesitated as she reached to check the pockets. She didn't want to invade their privacy, but she also didn't want to stick something in the wash that could ruin the clothes or worse yet, the machine.

Cautiously, she checked the pockets of the jeans. Empty. She breathed a sigh of relief as she stuck them in the washing machine's tub. She checked the next pair. She found the folded note she'd left for Mindy.

"Thank You again, Lord," she whispered as she put the jeans in the tub.

The next pair of jeans was grubbier than the others. Tyler's, she thought. Wary, she checked the pockets. She found some change, a guitar pick and a stack of small square sheets of thin paper that she recognized from her days on the streets. Zig-Zags. Used legally to roll tobacco cigarettes. Used illegally to roll a joint.

She tossed the squares away. This wasn't enough proof to convict Tyler of using. But it did indicate he bore watching closely. At least she hadn't found a syringe or a pouch of cocaine. She threw the jeans in the wash.

A little while later, she was bustling around the kitchen making popcorn when Nick came up behind her. Though he didn't touch her, she felt his regard like a warm caress. "You're good with them."

She turned and found herself one popcorn bowl's length between them. "I know what they need."

"Because you were once one of them?" his low, deep voice washed over her, drenching her senses.

She knew he wouldn't let it lie. "Yes. Because I once was a runaway."

He leaned closer, pressing the bowl into her ribs. "Why didn't you tell me before?"

Her mouth went dry. "I...I don't know."

His whiskered jaw tightened. "Tell me now."

She heard the footsteps of the teens coming down the stairs. "Not now."

The two boys entered the living room. They stopped when they saw Claire and Nick in the kitchen. She called to them. "There's a stack of movies in the video case. Why don't you two pick a good one we can all watch?"

She turned back to Nick and smiled brightly. "Come watch a movie with us."

His lip curled. "I'd rather not." He grabbed a handful of popcorn and left through the back door.

Once again.

Claire sighed.

Chapter Eleven

A noise awoke Nick from a nightmare. Sweat trickled down his forehead. He wiped it away as the images of Claire, hurt and bleeding, faded from his mind, leaving him uneasy.

He didn't like the idea of the teens so close.

A quick glance at the clock gave him a pretty good idea who had made the noise. 3:00 a.m. Claire's nocturnal wanderings. But he didn't trust the teenagers, so he got up. After pulling on his jeans and a T-shirt, he left his room.

He stopped in front of Mindy's room and listened. Nothing. He moved to the door of the room the two boys shared. Silence.

He'd heard Gwen return from work hours ago. No light shone from beneath her door.

Downstairs, Claire, dressed in light gray sweat pants and a U of O sweatshirt, was curled up on the bright yellow beanbag chair with a book in her hands and a small pool of light spilling over her from the standing lamp.

She looked up as he approached, her eyes wide, lips parted in surprise. "I didn't mean to wake you."

"You didn't." He sat next to her on the couch. "Have you always had trouble sleeping or is it me being here?"

Her gaze softened. "I've always suffered from insomnia. Reading helps me relax enough to go back to sleep."

He wouldn't allow himself to think about Claire relaxed and sleepy. "What are you reading?"

She held up the book so he could read the cover. A majestic castle surrounded by rolling green hills set off center of a couple, dressed in medieval garb, gazing into each other's eyes. The titled slashed across the top in gold script. Something to do with the Highlands.

She smiled. "A romance. My aunt got me hooked on them."

Fanciful stuff. Serena had enjoyed medical thrillers. "My mom and Lucy read those." He leaned forward. Telling himself he was just trying to help, he offered, "When my mom can't sleep, my dad rubs her shoulders. Most times that's where people hold their tension."

She held his gaze. "Really?"

"Really." He was standing in quicksand and sinking fast. But as he stared into her eyes, saw her wariness and a glimmer of interest, he realized he'd gladly dive in headfirst if in doing so he could give back to her a tenth of what she gave out.

She'd amazed him yet again this evening when

she'd clucked over those three lost chicks upstairs like a mother hen. Oozing maternal nurturing and kindness, yet firm in the way she dealt with them. Seeing to their needs without being condescending.

She hadn't even chastised him for his gruff refusal to participate in the dinner she'd prepared or to watch TV with them as if this were a normal situation for them all. It hadn't sat well with him.

She should have expected, demanded, more from him. Not that he would have given it. He didn't know what to make of her or his jumbled-up emotions about her. Rubbing her shoulders, touching her no matter how innocent his intentions, would be tantamount to playing with matches. They could both get burned. He wouldn't allow himself to be affected by her in any way. And if he repeated that often enough to himself it had to be true.

Right?

He cleared his throat. "On second thought, maybe hot chocolate would be good."

Claire stirred milk in a pot at the stove on medium heat with a wooden spoon. She hummed softly to herself as she watched Nick measure out generous scoops of powdered chocolate mix into two large mugs. They moved around the kitchen in such a cohesive way, as if they'd been doing it for years. She enjoyed the comfortable and relaxed way he made her feel, yet it made her heart ache with a yearning. She forced the feeling away, because yearning, hoping, expecting, were all bad news for her.

"Tell me what happened after your parents divorced."

She stiffened, and stopped humming. Tension gathered between her shoulder blades. The need to share welled up like a geyser about to blow. Would he understand? Could he? Would it change anything? Maybe. Maybe she could make him understand that the teens needed compassion and mercy.

Resuming her stirring, she started at the beginning. "My parents were young, still in high school, when my mother got pregnant with me."

Her voice sounded hollow, detached to her own ears. "They married. My dad took a job on the docks. My mother resented being stuck at home with a baby. She never let me forget that I was a mistake, unwanted. My dad tolerated me as long as I stayed out of the way. I became very good at staying out of the way."

Slowly, he turned to stare at her. "They were abusive?"

Her mouth twisted with bitter humor. "Depends what you consider abusive. Did they lock me in a closet? Tie me to a chair? Break my bones? No. I had food on my plate and a roof over my head."

Her throat tightened with memory, but she forced herself to remain detached. Only one way to find out if Nick could handle her past. "I bounced back and forth for a while between them. My mother changed everything about herself—her hair, her clothes and her job. She met a doctor and they got married the next year.

"My dad wanted to take a job on a fishing boat in

Alaska, something he'd always talked about, but because the custody agreement stated he had to have me half of each month, he couldn't. And he blamed me.

"I hated the bobbing back and forth. Hated them for not wanting me." She stopped, afraid she sounded whiny. Self-pity had no place in her life.

His hand covered hers around the spoon. She looked into his face and saw only tenderness in his eyes. Her spirit felt cared for, her tongue felt loose. Extracting her hand from beneath his, she moved to a cupboard and brought out a jar of cinnamon, giving herself a moment to gather her courage to finish her tale. "On my fourteenth birthday, my parents fought over who had to have me. I think they thought I wanted a party or something." She blew out a mocking breath and moved to where the mugs sat on the counter. "I told my parents a friend from school had invited me to her house for the weekend. They were ecstatic."

The bitterness crept into her voice despite her attempt not to let herself become emotional. As if she could rid herself of the past, she gave a violent shake of the spice jar, dumping the rust-colored powder into each mug. In her peripheral vision, she was aware of Nick as he came to stand beside her. He put the pot of steaming milk on a trivet on the counter and then stepped closer.

He slid her hair to the side and lightly brushed his fingertips on her shoulder. "Stray cinnamon," he murmured.

She set the jar down. "Thank you."

Her breath hitched as she felt a featherlight kiss on her head. Tears burned at the back of her throat.

His breath, warm and minty, fanned over her cheek. "Did you go to a friend's?"

Afraid to say the rest, she shook her head. His knuckles grazed her jawline. "You're so beautiful, Claire. Not just the outside, but inside where it matters."

Tears sprang to her eyes at his words. "I ran away."

"Ahh, sweet Claire," he said. His mouth hovered close to her cheek. If she turned her head a little, she could find his lips with her own. She held herself still.

"Tell me," he coaxed before his lips grazed her cheek. She closed her eyes against the torture of having him so close, so within reach, yet so unreachable.

"Uh-huh." The negative response was all she could manage.

He shifted, but then she realized he'd captured her hand and was tugging her close. She kept her gaze downcast.

"Did you run away to your aunt's?"

She shook her head and dropped her forehead to his chest. "My parents didn't miss me for two weeks. From what I was told they started asking around for me, but it was a good month before they contacted the authorities. By then I was in Seattle. A year later, I…"

She closed eyes against the memories. "I lived on the streets, dug through trash looking for food, begged from anyone who looked my way."

She'd gone this far, she might as well tell the rest. "I hooked up with a guy I thought needed me. But he didn't. I was the one who needed him. I made a bad choice. Several, really. I gave him my heart, my body. Allowed myself to get sucked into drugs."

She made a face as shame washed over her. "By the grace of God I never became addicted. The place where…where my boyfriend and I were staying was raided. He escaped and I was picked up by the police. The female officer took an interest in me when my parents didn't want me back. She contacted Aunt Denise, who took me in."

"Did you ever see your boyfriend again?"

"No."

He brought her captured hand up between them and slid his other arm around her back. She let her shame dissolve as she relaxed into him; his heart beat music in her ear. God had forgiven her for her foolishness even though she had a hard time forgiving herself.

It felt so good to be held, to have human contact. She understood why God had said it wasn't good for mankind to be alone. Human touch could bring peace and comfort.

Nick's deep voice filled the air as he began to softly sing. She melted further into his arms. She recognized the song. It was one of her favorites from Michael W. Smith's *Worship* album. She let the words wash over her, agreeing in her spirit that God would draw her close and never let her go.

As Nick's voice faded with the last refrain of the song, she wanted to tell him how grateful she was for his presence, for his soothing voice, but she didn't want to shatter the quiet of the moment with words.

When he started with a new song, her heart contracted painfully in her chest. The simple lyrics of the worship song spoke deep to her soul. He sang the song through the way it was written, the way she'd sung it a thousand times. Then he sang it again and changed the words, inserting her name for the pronoun I, making the song a prayer for God to open the eyes of her heart. To show her His power and love.

The tenderness of the prayer moved her deeply. Tears streamed down her cheeks. The last word of the chorus hung in the air, then seemed to swirl away, leaving a peaceful silence that wrapped around Claire, making her feel safe and cared for.

She must have sniffled or something, because he eased back. With the calloused pads of his fingers, he raised her chin so their gazes met. There was compassion in his eyes and tenderness on his face.

And she knew what she wanted.

With her free hand she reached up to touch his strong jaw. His day's worth of stubble tickled her palm.

His eyes grew darker and his breath hitched. "Claire," he said, his voice hoarse and rife with warning.

Her head told her to heed the warning. Her heart told her to take the risk. For ten years she'd been listening to her head. Tonight she was going with her heart. She went on tiptoe, moving cautiously, because if he showed any sign that he wasn't receptive, she'd retreat.

Tentatively, she touched her lips to his, felt the firmness and warmth.

The kiss was one-sided.

Then he breathed out her name and his lips yielded, molding to hers. She lost herself in the embrace. The sensations ran through her, reminding her of the time she'd fallen out of a tree. Dizzy, free and breathless. Anticipating the crash.

With agonizing clarity, she felt him disengage, pulling away, leaving her to face the landing alone.

He dropped his forehead to hers. "You're too generous, Claire."

Then he stepped back, his gaze bleak, his expression grim. "I can't do this. You deserve so much better than this. Than me."

Claire didn't know what she deserved, but she certainly knew what she wanted.

Nick.

And that terrified her. Because wanting could only lead to needing, which in turn led to expectations. And she knew where expectations led.

To a place she had no intention of going.

Eventually Nick would leave. He'd made no promise to stay. She had no choice but to shore up her defenses around her heart.

Being vulnerable to anyone was not something she could allow.

Nick sat on the twin bed in his room and stared at the stark white wall, but all he could see was Claire. Her big blue eyes wide with trust and hope. Her pink lips parting.

Oh, man. He'd made a mess of things.

He wasn't in the market for hurt again. He'd had his quota, enough to last the rest of his days. The hole Serena's death left in his heart, his life, could never be filled.

He wasn't any closer to understanding why God had brought him to Claire. He'd thought he was here to protect her from the teens. And he'd done such a great job, they were sleeping next door. With a groan, he laid back and sought the oblivion of sleep.

The morning came way too early for Nick, and with it a deep need to move, to get on his bike and feel the rush of wind biting at his skin, to see the world as a blur of color rather than details.

He dressed, putting his riding gear back on. He needed to get away from Claire, from the teens and the constant torment of remembering.

He stepped into the hall. The doors of the other rooms were closed. Moving quietly, he headed toward the stairs. Just as he arrived at the landing and was about to step down, Gwen's door opened.

She blinked at him through a fiery mass of red hair that engulfed her impish face. "Hey," she said.

"Good morning," he replied in a low voice.

She hefted her book bag onto her shoulder and shut her door.

"After you," Nick said, indicating she should proceed him down the stairs.

Little Nick stirred inside his crate. Gwen stopped and scratched his little snout through the crate before going outside. Nick followed her out. "You off to school?"

"Yeah. It's chem day."

He raised a brow. "What are you studying to be?"

She adjusted the bag on her shoulder. "I'm going into medicine. Thought I'd be a doctor, but now I'm thinking a physician's assistant."

"Why?"

Intelligence glowed bright in her amber eyes. "Less headache. Still get to do the doctoring but don't have the whole business aspect to deal with. I just want to help people."

Interesting. Another runaway who wanted to turn around and help others. Nick silently saluted Aunt Denise for her influence on Claire and Gwen. He would have liked to have known the woman. "Do you need a ride to school?"

"Bus stop's just down the road. I can study on the way." She started walking. "See ya later."

"Later."

Nick walked around to the back of the building where he kept his bike and pushed it a half block down the road before starting the engine and roaring away.

Two hours later, he was back. Though he felt invigorated, he wasn't refreshed the way he usually was after a ride. His mind was heavy with thoughts of Serena and the runaways. And Claire.

He parked his bike and went inside. He stopped at the sight of the teens sitting quietly at the table eating breakfast. Claire bustled about the kitchen, her graceful movements unhurried, her hair flowing free about her shoulders catching glints of sunlight.

The whole scene squeezed at his heart. He'd once hoped for a family. For children sitting at his table, his wife welcoming him with a warm smile as she offered him food she'd lovingly prepared.

But that wasn't to be. God had let some kid take away his chance for that kind of life. Serena had been ripped away from him as punishment for his greed. There were moments when he wished he'd died instead of her.

But he wasn't dead. And this wasn't his family.

He hardened his heart against the uselessness of his thoughts and moved forward, his boots echoing on the hardwood floor.

Mindy's eyes widened and she quickly shifted her attention toward Claire as if seeking refuge from him. Johnny stilled, his fork frozen half to his mouth while his eyes widened. Tyler's thin shoulders stiffened but he made a grand show of ignoring Nick by shoveling in his food at a rapid pace as if Nick might swoop down on him and take his plate away.

If being the bad guy kept the teens in line, Nick would gladly fill the role.

Claire stood by the counter that divided the dining area from the kitchen. Her wide smile didn't reach her eyes or so much as waver as she assessed him. He resisted the urge to squirm.

She lifted a brow. "Breakfast?"

He couldn't sit with the kids, couldn't bring himself to share a meal with the source of his pain. He shook his head.

She held his gaze for a beat. He couldn't decipher the emotion lighting her eyes. She spun away. Her movements turned jerky, angry.

He frowned. Ignoring the teenagers and their now curious stares, he walked to Claire. He laid a hand on her shoulder, stilling her action. "Why are you angry?"

"I'm not angry. What makes you think I'm angry?"

She slammed the dishwasher door shut, rattling the dishes inside.

"Is this about our conversation last night?"

She turned on the faucet and scrubbed a pot. "No."

"Then what has you so upset?"

"Nothing." She turned off the faucet and dried her hands. "What are your plans, Nick?"

He narrowed his gaze. "My plans?"

She faced him squarely. "Plans. Like, are you staying or leaving?"

He glanced at the group huddled at the table, their avid gazes fixed on him. He didn't trust them, couldn't leave her to their mercy. "Staying."

"For how long?"

He didn't know.

Feeling like he was walking into a trap, he shrugged. "As long as needed."

A cold smile twisted her lips. "I don't need you."

His chin came up and he tried to belie the sting her words caused. "Until we figure out a game plan for them—" he jerked his thumb toward the teens "—I'm staying."

"Why?"

He leaned in close so only she'd hear his words. "I don't trust them."

She leaned closer still, her breath tickling his ear. "Let them earn your trust."

Her fresh scent assaulted his senses, stirring a yearning in him he'd just as soon not have. A yearning to taste her kiss again. To bury his hands in her hair and feel her soft skin rasping against his calloused hands. He straightened. She stepped back as color darkened her cheeks. Was she remembering their kiss?

He gave a negative shake of his head, not sure he was saying no to her statement or to his thoughts. Her gaze dropped but not before he saw the disappointment in her eyes. He didn't like the way her disappointment tempted him to relent.

Moving past him, she said to the teens, "When you're done eating, please take your plates to the sink." Then she walked through the living room and stomped upstairs, leaving Nick alone with three wary teenagers.

Now what was he supposed to do?

Claire took out her exasperation and frustration on the toilet bowl she was cleaning. Men!

When she'd awakened and found Nick gone, she'd assumed he left for good. Her heart had twisted in agony, but she told herself it was for the best. That a man with as much baggage as he carried would only drag her down.

But it had still hurt.

And she'd stuffed that ache down deep with all the other disappointments in her life and chastised herself for wishing he'd stay.

Then he just waltzed back in and she realized he'd only gone for a ride. She hated the joy that leapt in her soul. The joy turned quickly to anger directed at herself. When would she learn?

She finished the bathroom and went downstairs to make sure no mayhem had transpired after she'd left Nick alone with the three teenagers.

The teens were fine, she saw with relief. Mindy and Johnny were playing Ping-Pong and Tyler was slouched on the yellow beanbag watching TV. Little Nick was his constant companion.

"Where's Nick?" she asked.

"Out front," the boy named Johnny responded as he slammed a shot across the table.

Mindy deftly shot the white ball back at him.

Contentment unfurled inside Claire's chest. This was what she'd envisioned. Teenagers enjoying the place, feeling safe and secure. As time went on they would open up and trust her.

If only that would happen with Nick. But after this morning, she was too afraid to hope. For anything.

The days seemed to fly by. Claire couldn't believe how much work it was having three teens underfoot 24/7. Doing triple the amount of laundry. Triple the amount of food to feed three growing youths, plus a grown man. She felt like she spent half the week at the grocery store.

She hadn't realized how much Aunt Denise had done for her and Gwen. Or how self-sufficient Gwen had become over the years.

Claire kept expecting her bank account to run dry with all the extra expenses. But for some reason the bank's balance and her balance didn't match. The bank's balance was always higher. But she didn't have a spare moment to sit down and calculate the discrepancy.

On Sunday she took the teens to church with her. Though the teenagers had grumbled, she reminded them of her house rules. She was certain once they got involved in the youth group, they'd want to attend. Nick had shaken his head when she'd asked if he were going with them. But halfway through the service, she glanced back and there he was, leaning against the wall looking intimidating and imposing.

They never talked about his appearance at church. Or the fact that he stayed away from the teens. She'd thought after hearing her story and understanding why she wanted to help the teenagers, he'd have softened some. He hadn't. The few times she asked him about it, he deflected her questions. Very neatly. She realized he was good at that.

Four days before the auction, Claire, wearing her twill khakis and a striped shirt, headed outside in search of Nick. He was tinkering with his bike.

The three teens were out front, as well. Mindy threw the ball for Little Nick while Johnny hung close to Nick, watching him. Johnny seemed to do that a lot. She wondered if Nick noticed how much the boy wanted his attention. Tyler, on the other hand, stayed as far from Nick as possible. Nick didn't even try to hide the simmering anger in his eyes every time he looked at the kid.

Claire stopped next to Nick. He glanced over his

shoulder and then stood. His expression was welcoming. "Hi."

"Hi. I'm off to Sandy's."

Panic replaced the welcoming light in his eyes. "You're not leaving me alone with them."

She pursued her lips. Legally, she shouldn't since he wasn't an employee and wasn't licensed to provide care to anyone. But since The Zone wasn't officially open for business yet, she decided to consider the teenagers and Nick as guests.

She hoped to help them all reconcile with their parents, because deep inside she truly believed in the idea of family, but if reconciliation wasn't possible…well, she'd deal with that dilemma later.

She had to leave soon or she'd be late. "I'm confident you can handle things here. Find something for them to do."

She leaned closer so only he could hear. "Try to get them to open up to you."

His stricken look gave her a second's doubt about the wisdom of charging him with such a delicate task. "Pray. God will strengthen you," she whispered.

His nostrils flared and those dark eyes glared at her.

Claire backed up. "Hey, Mindy. Do you want to come with me?"

The girl's face lit up. "Sure."

Claire heart squeezed a bit. All these kids really wanted was someone to care.

But what about Nick?

Her gaze strayed to him. What did he want? And could she help him find it without losing herself in the process?

Chapter Twelve

"That's a good idea, Mindy," Claire declared with enthusiasm.

The young girl ducked her head with a pleased smile. Claire knew she'd made the right decision in bringing Mindy with her to the fund-raising committee meeting at Sandy's house.

They sat in the living room on blue chintz couches and matching overstuffed chairs. The soft taupe-colored walls coordinated well with the dark beige carpet. Like Sandy, the living room was well put together and cozy, evoking a sense of welcoming.

Lori, Sandy, Peggy Jordan and the pastor's wife, Mary, welcomed Mindy and kindly included her in the planning for the spring picnic basket auction.

Mindy blossomed under the warm regard of the ladies. She wasn't nearly as tentative as she'd been at first.

Anticipation mingled with anxiety in Claire. She

didn't want to hope for a lot, yet she couldn't quite muster up indifference. She wanted this event to be a success. Yet, she sternly told herself not to get her hopes up about the picnic because a fall from lofty heights always hurt.

As the ladies discussed the decorations, Claire thought about Nick and the two boys. He'd insisted on staying, so she'd decided to let him take some of the responsibility. And in truth, it was a relief to be able to take Mindy with her.

Away from Tyler's influence, Mindy might open up and say why she'd run away. Most people assumed kids ran away from some kind of abuse. Claire often found herself falling into that trap because of her own experience. But there were no telltale signs to watch for, no indicators that screamed abuse.

A kid could have been spoiled rotten by parents who never could get a handle on their child's behavior and when the parent finally set a boundary, the teen reacted. Some ran, some lashed out.

Or a good kid could get hooked up with the wrong type of friend. Peer pressure combined with hormones made for a crazy and sometimes dangerous mix.

Mindy seemed to have a good head on her shoulders. Claire had a feeling there was something ugly involved. Whatever it was, Claire would help Mindy deal with it.

"Thanks for coming with me today," Claire said on the way back to The Zone.

Mindy beamed. "I had a great time. Mrs. Wellington is so nice."

"Yes, she sure is. She and my aunt were best friends."

Silence met her comment. Claire thought through all the training she'd had, forming a plan to get Mindy to open up. She settled with a direct approach. "Does your mother have a friend like Mrs. Wellington?"

Mindy glanced over. "No."

"It's too bad she doesn't have anyone to lean on now that you're gone. She must be awfully lonely," Claire said in a conversational tone.

"She's got her boyfriend," Mindy muttered.

Claire winced at the bitter undertones. "You jealous?"

Mindy scoffed. "I hate that pig."

Now they were getting somewhere. Claire kept her tone low, unthreatening. "Does he hurt your mother?"

Mindy shrugged and turned away.

"Has he hurt you?"

When she didn't answer, Claire gripped the steering wheel. *Stay calm.* She didn't want to push too hard and lose what little ground she'd gained. "No one has the right to hurt another person. Especially when they're bigger and stronger."

Still silence. Claire tried another tactic. A personal one. "My father used his fists when he'd get angry or drunk. Or both." She shuddered at the memories assaulting her. Thankfully, time and distance had lessened the impact of her childhood.

Several minutes stretched by before Mindy shifted. Her shoulders shook and Claire realized the girl was silently crying. Claire quickly maneuvered the car through the traffic and entered the parking lot of the local elementary school. She stopped and turned off the car.

She put a hand on Mindy's shoulder, offering her comfort. The young girl swiveled around, allowing Claire to put an arm across her thin shoulders. Words tumbled out of Mindy.

Claire hung on to both the girl and her own repulsion as the nature of the abuse became apparent. Her mother's boyfriend hadn't hit her, he'd molested her.

Sickened and angry, Claire found her voice. "Did you tell your mother?"

Mindy wiped a hand across her nose. "She didn't believe me. She said I must have misunderstood what he did." Mindy's eyes pleaded with Claire. "It wasn't right what he did to me."

"No, honey, it wasn't right. Your mama needs to know exactly what happened." Claire resolved to make it right even if she had to drag the boyfriend to jail herself.

Claire started the car and headed back to The Zone. She needed to talk about what she found out, needed help processing the information. For the first time since her aunt's death there was someone whom she wanted to confide in.

Nick.

Nick squatted next to his Harley. With a rag he wiped down the pipes, bringing the chrome to a gleaming shine. It was an excuse, really—something to do while keeping an eye on the two teens.

He'd set them to weeding the yard. Amazingly, Tyler had only rolled his eyes once before doing as instructed. Johnny, Nick discovered, was eager to please. The boy had finished one section and asked for an inspection. Warily, Nick had gone to check out the boy's work.

"Good job," he'd commented and noted with mild surprise the pleasure lighting up the boy's eyes at the simple praise. It made Nick wonder more about the boy, made him mad that he wondered.

He paused as he heard quiet footsteps behind him. He glanced over his shoulder.

Johnny stood there. His eyes devoured the bike, reminding Nick of his own youth when he'd been fascinated with motorcycles but his mother had put the kibosh on having one any time he'd brought up the subject. The first thing he'd done when he'd graduated from college was buy his dream bike.

"Cool bike," Johnny said when he met Nick's gaze.

"That it is." Nick stood, wiped his hands on his jeans. His gaze swept the area, stopping on the target of his search. Tyler had moved to the area around one of the laurel bushes.

"What's it like to ride?"

Nick brought his gaze back to Johnny. "It's pretty cool."

Johnny nodded, his eyes gleaming with wistfulness. Nick averted his gaze. "My dad had a bike. Not nearly as tricked out as yours but it was cool. I never got a chance to ride on it."

Nick frowned, not liking the twinge of understanding running through him. "Did your mom make your dad get rid of it?"

The light in the kid's eyes dimmed. "No. Mom was okay with the bike." The kid shrugged. "Dad just took off on it one day and never came back."

That grabbed Nick's attention. "How long ago?"

Johnny shrugged. "A year or so."

Nick saw the burn of pain in Johnny's eyes that said he wasn't as nonchalant as he sounded. Nick would've bet the kid knew exactly how many days, if not hours, his father had been gone. Nick didn't even try for tact and went for the obvious. "And your mother? Did she beat you?"

"Mom? No." Johnny kicked at the dirt, his gaze now downcast.

Nick really didn't want to know. Didn't want to care. *Not my concern.* But for Claire's sake he asked, "Then why'd you take off?"

Johnny jammed his hands into his front pockets. With his shoulders hunched, he looked even younger than sixteen. "Easier on Mom."

Nick raised a brow. "Easier, how?"

Johnny slanted a quick glance in Tyler's direction, before replying, "She's got my two sisters to look after plus her job at the bank. I just was in the way."

Nick crossed his arms over his chest. "Does she even know you're alive?"

"Huh? Of course."

"So you've talked to her since you ran off."

The kid frowned. "Well. No. But I mean…"

Nick shook his head in disgust. "Man, you need

to call her. Let her know she only needs to be mourning your absence, not your death."

By the horrified expression in Johnny's eyes, Nick guessed the boy never thought about his mother thinking the worst. Nick inclined his head. "The phone's waiting."

Johnny spun on his heels and raced inside, slamming the door behind him.

Nick let out a heavy breath. *Andrews, you're a hypocrite.* Time to break out that stationery Claire had given him. But what would he say to his parents?

The hairs on the back of Nick's nape rose a split second before he heard Tyler demand, "What'd ya do to Johnny?"

Nick pivoted to face Tyler. The teen's eyes glittered angrily. His hands were fisted and jittery. Nick narrowed his gaze. Interesting. Tyler was ready to brawl with him in defense of Johnny. Maybe runaways had their own code of honor. Nick could respect that. Even though looking at the kid stirred up painful memories, igniting the anger that never seemed to extinguish itself.

Nick wasn't about to defend himself to Tyler, nor was he going to break Johnny's confidence by revealing what they'd talked about. Really, he'd just as soon Tyler took a swing at him. But knowing that it would upset Claire, he deliberately relaxed his stance and shrugged. "When you gotta go, you gotta go."

Tyler's challenging gaze wavered slightly with doubt.

Nick diverted his attention. "Since you're so good at painting, I have some signs that need to be made."

Nick walked away and a few seconds later Tyler
followed. Nick explained to him what they were after. Signs to advertise the spring picnic basket auction.

Tyler gave a curt nod before organizing the supplies. Nick watched with interest the way he lined
each can of paint up, laid out the different-size poster
board that Claire had brought home one day last
week. The kid seemed to be assessing the situation,
approaching it like a puzzle.

Tyler glanced over his shoulder. "What?"

Nick held up his hands, palms out. "Nothing. I'll
be in the house if you have a problem."

Tyler turned back to his task as if Nick had already disappeared.

Nick walked inside with a frown. He didn't get
that kid. Didn't want to. All he had to do was remember Serena, and that a punk like the one out front
killed her. He wasn't going to let anything bad happen to Claire.

Johnny was sitting at the counter with the phone
to his ear. From the pained expression on his young
face, Nick surmised the conversation with Johnny's
mother was pretty heavy.

"Yeah, Mom. I know. I'm sorry." Johnny dropped
his head into his free hand. "Aw, Mom, don't cry
again. I'm okay. I'm here at this…" Johnny looked
at Nick.

Nick nodded his encouragement.

"I'm at this shelter place. In Pineridge. No,
Mom. Please." Johnny rolled his eyes. "They're
real nice here." He listened for a few moments.

"Okay, hold on." He held the phone away from his ear and grimaced. "She, uh, wants to talk with you."

Nick's solar plexus spasmed, forcing the air from his lungs as effectively as a punch to the gut. He wasn't qualified to speak to the mother of a runaway. Where was Claire? He slowly took the phone. "Hello?"

"I sure hope this is legitimate because if it isn't, I'll have you in jail so fast your head will spin. I want my son home," the female voice on the other end of the line snarled.

A mama bear defending her cub. Obviously, she hadn't considered her son a burden. Nick cleared his throat. "Mrs...?" He looked expectantly at Johnny.

"Kent," Johnny supplied.

"Kent," Mrs. Kent snapped at the same time.

Nick took a deep breath. "Mrs. Kent. The Zone is a teen shelter run by Claire Wilcox. She—"

"I want to speak to her," Mrs. Kent interrupted.

"She's in a meeting at the moment but the second she is able, I will have her call you."

"Well, who are you?"

Grimacing, Nick wasn't sure how to answer that. "I...I help out Claire."

"How do I know you haven't kidnapped my son for some depraved purpose?"

He could tell she was working herself up. He tried for a soothing tone. "Why don't you contact the Pineridge Police Department? Ask for Officer Bob Grand. He will vouch for The Zone."

"Believe me, I will."

The sound of the front door opening brought welcome relief. Nick waved Claire over with a sharp flick of his wrist.

Into the phone he said, "Could you hold on one moment, please?" He covered the mouthpiece with his hand as Claire approached, her eyes questioning. "Johnny's mother."

Claire's eyes went wide and a soft "Ohhh," escaped her parted lips. Her gaze swung to Johnny. He gave her a half smile and half grimace.

Still holding his hand over the mouthpiece, Nick extended the phone to her. "You've got to reassure her that he's okay and explain who you are. Her name's Mrs. Kent."

Claire's eyes narrowed. "What's the scoop?"

Not waiting for Johnny to respond, Nick explained, "He ran because his dad took off. Thought his mom and sisters would be better off without another mouth to feed. His mom's not so happy."

Without batting an eye, she took the phone. "Hello, Mrs. Kent. My name is Claire Wilcox and I run The Zone, a teen shelter here in Pineridge."

Winded as if he'd run the New York City marathon, Nick left Claire to her work and headed for his bike. Johnny wasn't such a bad kid, after all.

Score one for Claire and The Zone.

The back roads on the outskirts of Pineridge were becoming familiar to Nick. He'd found a mile-long stretch of flat road where he could wind up the engine and let go full throttle. Though the road wasn't a curved track and there were no fans cheering, he felt the same exhilarating rush of adrenaline as if he were flat-track racing.

Short-lived.

Temporary.

Unlike Claire.

There was nothing temporary about her. She was the kind of girl his mother would approve of. The kind of woman Serena would have liked. The kind of woman who deserved forever.

He didn't have forever in him. Not anymore.

He took comfort in knowing he'd been up-front with her. Neither one of them had illusions that he was staying for good.

He parked his bike near the front cement stairs leading into The Zone. The most heavenly smell drifted out the door as he walked in. The scents of savory spices evoked memories of family dinners. All the laughter, the contentment. He yearned for hearth and home. Things he'd denied himself for the past two years.

Little Nick barked as he raced to greet him. Nick petted the dog. Dodging wet kisses, Nick realized the small animal had worked its way into his heart. Better a puppy than a blue-eyed blonde.

Claire paused in the act of serving dinner. Her hair was caught back in a barrette at the nape of her graceful neck. Her jeans embraced her gentle curves. A flash of skin showed at her midriff where her tank top rose as she leaned forward to dish out the wonderful-smelling casserole in her hands. The warmth in her eyes and her smile trapped the air in his lungs.

"Hello." Her greeting was equally warm. "Have a good ride?"

"I did." The invigorating ride had cleared his head and his heart for a moment. He savored such moments. "That smells wonderful."

She grinned wider. "Hopefully it will taste good. Mindy and I made it up."

His gaze raked over the three teenagers sitting at the table. Tyler had his elbows on the tabletop, his face averted from Nick. Johnny poured himself some milk. Mindy gave him a tentative smile. "That was nice of you to help out," Nick said to the young girl.

Her smiled grew and she ducked her head.

Claire patted his arm. "Go wash up."

He shrugged out of his leather jacket and hung it on the coatrack by the front door, then went to wash his hands. When he came out of the bathroom, he noticed Gwen had joined the group at the table. A thick braid hung down her back and an open textbook lay in her lap. She glanced up as he approached and waved a quick greeting before returning her attention to her book. Claire handed him a full plate of casserole, salad and bread and offered him a fork and a napkin.

"Thank you," he said.

"What would you like to drink?"

"A bottle of water would be great." He tracked her movements to the fridge, his gaze drinking in the sight of her. She came back and handed him a cold bottle. On the outside of the plastic container, her prints showed in the condensation. Small, delicate hands.

She sat at the table, leaving him standing alone. He was tired of being alone.

Tonight he would join Claire's world. He just hoped he survived the visit.

He sat in the empty chair and enjoyed the surprised look on Claire's pretty face. "So, what happened while I was out?"

She looked at him, her expression the epitome of bliss. "Nothing."

Sunset filled The Zone with radiant rays of orange and gold that shone through the windows, casting long shadows across the furniture as Claire descended the stairs. The Zone was finally quiet after the ruckus of dinner and TV. Now the kids were safely tucked in bed.

Interestingly enough, Tyler's response to her mothering wasn't what she expected. She'd thought he'd rebel with loud words and angry actions when she came in to say lights out. He'd scowled at her fiercely, turned over and faced the wall without another word. Obviously, his gruff demeanor was a defense against the world. That gave her hope. He wasn't unredeemable.

She still couldn't get over Nick joining her and the teens for dinner at the table. The atmosphere had been reasonably amicable. Nick had drawn Johnny out with talk of motorcycles. Mindy had even ventured into the conversation. Gwen had closed her book and engaged, as well. The only blight had been Tyler's smart-mouthed comments and Nick's smoldering anger every time he looked at the boy.

But she wouldn't let that ruin the good that had been done that day. She was ecstatic that Nick had done way beyond what she could have ever expected or hoped with Johnny.

Admiration and affection unfurled in her chest. Nick had somehow managed to get Johnny to not only open up, but to call and reconcile with his mother. It took a man relating to a young man to accomplish that. She was so thankful Johnny's history didn't include abuse and neglect. Just a misguided attempt to help his mother.

A soft glow illuminated the window in the new back door. She headed in that direction and peeked through the door's square, curtainless window.

Nick sat on the top stair, his shoulders hunched. Little Nick lay beside him chewing on a bone. Her brows drew together until she realized Nick was furiously writing on the stationery she'd given him.

Yes! She couldn't help the satisfied grin on her face. This was an important step in mending whatever broken fence separated Nick from his parents. She was so proud of him. Now, if she could only ferret out his dreams.

Claire moved away from the window. She didn't want Nick to think she was spying on him. She sat on the couch, slipped off her shoes and tucked her feet beneath her. Closing her eyes, she silently talked with God, telling him about the day and how grateful she was for all of His blessings.

A little while later, the back door opened and Nick stepped in. His presence filled The Zone with the contrasting elements of calmness and energy. Her senses went on heightened alert. Awareness like a homing beacon tracked him to the living room.

Little Nick leapt onto the couch and into her lap, licking at her face. "Oh, yes, I love you, too," she said while dodging his kisses.

Nick sat on the couch a mere cushion's space away. Her pulse quickened. His scent, masculine and clean, enveloped her as she breathed in.

"So...quite the day," he said, his voice a low rumble she felt in her chest.

She set Little Nick back on the floor while trying to control her attraction to Nick. "Yes. It's been an amazing day. For both of us." She proceeded to tell him about Mindy's revelations. Every time her gaze met his, her heart skipped a beat.

Nick whistled low through his teeth. "That's rough. What are you going to do?"

She plucked a lint ball from the edge of the couch and rolled it between her index finger and her thumb. "Contact the proper authorities and her mother." She grimaced, knowing the battle that lay ahead. "I'm praying her mom will wake up and see the truth."

"Are you sure she's telling the truth?" he asked as he stretched an arm across the back of the couch.

"Yes. I believe her." She studied his arresting face. His strong jaw, shadowed by a manly beard, made her itch to feel the burn of his whiskers. His tanned skin stretched taut over his finely sculpted cheekbones. Those dark eyes that entranced her. She enjoyed looking at him.

He reached for her hair, gently twining a lock through his fingers. The intimacy of the gesture caught her off guard with a jolt. She fought back the urge to scoot closer and snuggle up against him. Like a married couple.

She swallowed. "I...I promised Mrs. Kent I'd bring Johnny home tomorrow. They live about forty-five minutes away in Beaverton. The poor woman was beside herself with worry. She'd thought something horrible had happened to him. In this day and age, I don't blame her."

Nick nodded empathetically. "If you don't mind, I'll take Johnny home."

"Really?" Claire tucked her chin and stared at Nick. A little dumbfounded with surprise, she said, "Uh, sure. You know where my keys are."

A mischievous gleam entered his eyes. "I think the bike would be better."

"Oh." Understanding dawned. Tenderness exploded in her chest. "Much better. He'll be thrilled."

Nick grinned and her heart thumped against her ribs with all kinds of hopes and needs and wants. But she couldn't muster up her defenses. Nick was systematically removing the barricade she'd erected around her heart without even realizing he was doing so. She was going to have to find some cement left within her to resist his powerful pull.

Obviously, there were some lessons she had trouble learning.

Chapter Thirteen

The next morning dawned with dark clouds threatening rain. Spring in Oregon. One minute nice and temperate and then the next moment the rains appeared, giving the soil and vegetation a cleansing drink. Though the state needed the rainwater to keep the greenery lush, Claire didn't like the idea of Nick and Johnny astride a motorcycle on wet pavement.

The mood was somber as Johnny said his goodbyes. Mindy sniffed back tears but smiled gamely as she hugged her friend.

Tyler's hooded eyes observed everything from where he stood at the bottom of the stairs. He didn't come close and wish Johnny well. "Whatever," had been his response to Johnny's earlier goodbye.

Claire gave Tyler a worried glance. For all his supposed indifference, he had to be feeling something. She looked back to where Johnny was climbing on the back of Nick's bike with a huge grin. The helmet Claire had worn fit the boy well.

Her gaze locked with Nick's. Her own concern reflected in his eyes. Would Tyler act out over this? She squared her shoulders and gave Nick a quick shake of her head and mouthed, "It'll be okay." She was confident she could deal with whatever Tyler tried to dish out.

Nick's eyes narrowed as he looked from her to Tyler and back. "You call Bob if you need anything. I'll be back in a few hours."

She should have bristled at his protectiveness. Instead, she found it touching. "I will. You be careful." She glanced up at the swollen clouds.

"A little rain won't hurt," Nick murmured.

She nodded, taking his assurance at face value. Of course, he'd have ridden in the rain before. She hugged Johnny one last time then squeezed Nick's arm.

His lopsided grin made her lungs stall. Then he started the motorcycle. The rhythmic rumble vibrated right through her. "I never got my second promised ride."

"When I come back."

She grinned. "I'll hold you to that."

He and Johnny rode away. Claire watched until they were out of sight, her heart squeezing slightly. She sighed. Oh, baby. She was in deep trouble, because already she missed Nick and couldn't wait for him to return.

Expectations only lead to disappointments.

It's okay to have feelings for people, Sandy had said.

Her feelings for Nick were complicated and unclear. She wasn't ready to examine them too closely. She didn't know if she ever would be.

"Claire?"

Mindy's voice pulled Claire from her thoughts. Gathering her weak resolve to not hope for anything from Nick, she focused her attention on the young girl.

"Yes?"

"Will you call my mom?"

With a smile, Claire looped her arm around Mindy. Pride that she was helping the girl so soon filled her chest. They walked inside together with Tyler bringing up the rear, and Claire was glad to have something else to concentrate on other than her growing feelings toward Nick.

Feelings that terrified her.

Claire first informed social services of the crime against Mindy and then called Mindy's mother. The conversation turned heated. Shari Vaughn didn't want to believe her daughter had been molested. It wasn't uncommon for parents of molested children to resist the truth because in acknowledging what had happened, they had to admit they'd been unable to protect their child.

Mindy had been reluctant to talk with her mother and Claire hadn't pressed. She assured the girl they weren't giving up. It would take time.

Mindy retreated to her room. Tyler lounged in front of the T.V. with Little Nick in his lap. Wanting to give Mindy space and not up to the challenge of delving into Tyler's psyche, Claire decided to do laundry.

After changing her own sheets, she took a fresh set of twin sheets out of the cupboard in the bathroom and went to Nick's room.

As had become her routine on every third day, she laid the fresh linens on the corner of his neatly made bed. She knew tomorrow she'd find the dirty sheets piled tidily on the floor by the door. She tried not to think about how uncomfortable he probably was sleeping on the twin mattress. Not once had he complained.

She went down the stairs with her load. As she passed the coatrack by the front door an envelope lying on the floor caught her attention. A piece from the stationery she'd given Nick. She snatched up the envelope. It was sealed and addressed to Mr. and Mrs. Andrews, Long Island, New York. It must have fallen from his jacket pocket.

Whatever rift lay between him and his parents wouldn't be healed with him clear on the other side of the country. His parents deserved to know he was alive and well. They deserved to know what he'd written.

She dropped the basket off in the laundry room and went to her desk where she put a stamp on the corner of the envelope. Stacking Nick's letter with her other out-going mail, she was confident Nick would thank her later.

The late afternoon sun appeared after the morning showers. The golden rays brought steam rising from the leaves of the plants and heightened the scent of moist earth. Claire loved to breathe in the fresh, crisp air after a rain shower. She stood on the new back porch contemplating how a patio table and chairs would fit on the square expanse of wood.

She heard the low rumble of Nick's motorcycle. Her heart did a little thump in her chest as he rounded the corner on the paved path, stopping his bike close to the porch steps.

He smiled. "Are you ready for that ride?"

Excitement bubbled and pulsed in her veins. Yes, she wanted to sit close to Nick and wrap her arms around his waist as the wind whipped by. But she couldn't. She shook her head as she quelled the rebellious chorus of groans going on in her head. "I can't."

He raised a brow. "Why not?"

"I can't leave." But, oh, she'd like to.

"We won't go far." The smoothness of his deep voice contrasted with the rough rumbling of his Harley.

"What if they need something?" She had to be there for the teens. She'd brought them to The Zone—she couldn't go off and play, leaving them alone.

He contemplated her for a moment. "How about we ride around the park? I'll even let you drive," his silky voice challenged.

His suggestion sent her pulse spinning. "I wouldn't know the first thing about driving one of these."

He held out the extra helmet. "It's easy. Like driving a car." His eyes took on a roguish gleam. "Besides, I'm not going to let you ride this alone."

She still hesitated.

"Come on, Claire. You deserve to play," he coaxed.

"We'll stay close by?" The eagerness in her voice betrayed her inner conflict.

His infectious grin was irresistible and drew her down the stairs. "We'll never lose sight of the building."

Heady anticipation had her reaching for the helmet. She slid it on her head and buckled the clasp under her chin. Nick scooted back and patted the seat in front of him. She swallowed down her giddy excitement and tried for decorum, but couldn't stop the silly grin on her face.

She climbed on the Harley and looked over her shoulder at him, waiting for her lesson. His broad chest rested against her back as he leaned forward. He guided her hands to the handlebars. His big, warm hands closed over hers on the black grips, making concentration difficult.

"Right hand has the front brakes. Squeeze gently," his deep voice intoned, causing her to shiver at the thrill of sitting so close, so intimately with him. He applied pressure to her hand and demonstrated the squeezing of the brake lever.

"Left hand works the clutch." Again he demonstrated with her hand trapped beneath his—she ridiculously felt sheltered and secure.

With his right foot, he nudged her foot onto the pedal. "Rear brake. When you brake to stop, use both in tandem. Rear brake won't completely stop you and the front alone will send you flying over the handlebars."

She absorbed that. She had no wish to go head over heels onto the pavement.

He reached down and tucked her left foot under a small bar. When he straightened, he said, "Left foot works the gears. We'll stay in first. Squeeze the clutch and press your foot down at the same time just like in a car. Right hand twists the throttle back slightly until you're ready to open her up."

"Whoa. Much more complicated than I'd imagined." She tried to remember his instructions.

He laughed. "You'll do fine." He shifted on the seat behind her. "You ready?" he asked, his breath tickling her exposed neck below the helmet.

Trepidation hammered in her ears. She nodded.

"Okay. Clutch, gear, throttle."

She tried the sequence. She usually didn't have a problem with coordination, but as she pressed and squeezed and twisted she felt awkward and clumsy. The bike lurched and died. Her heart jumped in her throat. Nick's laugh vibrated against her back. He started the engine again.

She glanced back at him. The enjoyment on his face and the encouragement in his eyes affected her deeply. This man had brought so much into her life. So much she hadn't realized was missing. He'd brought fun, joy and companionship when for so long her life had been about achieving her goal. About staying safely behind her walls.

"Try again," he said.

She blew out a breath. Okay. She could do this. How hard could it really be? She tried again. The bike lurched but didn't die this time.

"Throttle," Nick's voice commanded.

"Oh, yeah. All three. At the same time. Right."

She tried again, this time rolling the rubber-coated throttle back as she worked the clutch and the gear. They moved forward, startling her into squeezing the front brake. The sudden jarring stop bounced her on the seat.

Nick's arm came around her waist, steadying her.

"Again," he said.

She tried again. Again. And again until she thought she'd scream with frustration. Sweat trickled down her neck. Then, finally, she managed to coordinate her limbs and they moved slowly forward.

"Take us to the road," Nick suggested.

She did. Nick let her be in control as she drove the Harley down the street. When they came to the intersection, he leaned closer, pressing himself flat against her as he helped her steer the bike in a wide arc. He released his hands from her and straightened. Cool air rushed between them as she drove the bike back down the street.

"Use both brakes when you're ready to slow and stop," he instructed.

She pressed with her foot and squeezed with her hand and they slowed to a stop in front of The Zone. Gwen, Mindy and Tyler stood on the front porch. Gwen and Mindy clapped and ran down the walkway to them. Tyler remained on the porch, his arms crossed over his chest and a bored expression on his face.

Claire reached up and took off the helmet. She met Nick's glittering gaze. "That was fun."

"Yes. It was." The underlying tone lacing his words captivated her. Made her aware of herself as a woman and him as a man. A couple. Her heart stalled.

"Can I have a ride?" Mindy asked, her eyes wide and her expression eager.

Grateful for the intrusion of reality, Claire slipped from the seat. Nick scooted forward on the seat and indicated for Mindy to climb on the back. He took her for a ride around the park.

"You two are good together," Gwen commented.

Claire tracked Nick. "We're...friends."

"Right."

At the disbelief in Gwen's tone, Claire shifted her gaze to the young woman at her side. "Really. We're just friends."

Gwen's jewel-colored eyes twinkled. "If you say so." She checked her watch. "Ohhh, got to go get ready for work." She disappeared inside.

Claire returned her attention to Nick. There couldn't ever be anything more between them. Could there?

She turned her mind away from that thought. There was no use in hoping, expecting more. Life didn't work that way. Not for her.

The last few days before the auction were a whirlwind of activity, with people coming and going from The Zone. Claire felt like a revolving door. The fundraising committee worked endlessly on publicity and decorations.

Pastor Gary offered his services as the auctioneer. Bob stopped by several times offering his help, but Claire knew he was keeping an eye on Nick as well as the teens. Bob had made a habit of checking in ever since Mrs. Kent had called him.

Tyler was still sullen and uncommunicative. Claire noticed he had a certain artistic flare that came out in the most simple of paint projects. He'd done a great job on the signs for the auction.

She'd tried to talk to him about his creativity, but he'd shot her down with a smart remark before withdrawing to his corner of the living room. She'd let it go. If she pushed he'd bolt altogether.

She'd resorted to asking Mindy if she knew anything about Tyler's background. She learned the boy's father was in prison for manslaughter, leaving him at the mercy of his crack-addicted mother, who used lit cigarettes and a thick belt to control her child. Tyler had been taken from his mother and placed in foster care. Mindy had shrugged and said that didn't work out so he ran. Claire's heart cried for Tyler. She had to figure out a way to help him.

The day of the auction arrived with a beautiful cloudless sky. The evergreen-scented air was ripe with anticipation that Claire felt deep in her bones. It seemed even the two teens felt the invigorating impatience. They rose early, dressed and helped Nick set up the chairs in the park across the street.

It had been decided to set up the auction in the park, using the gazebo for the auctioneer, with tables in front to display the many baskets.

Claire's own basket sat on the table with the other thirty-six baskets donated for the auction. She'd found a white wicker, oval-shaped basket with a high handle at the antique store in town. Mindy had helped her decorate it with purple ribbons and silk flowers.

For the fare inside, Claire had dug out some of her aunt's favorite recipes. Spicy fried chicken, dill-and-sour-cream potato salad, blueberry turnovers, hot-and-smoky baked beans and green apple slices with French brie. Gwen had also added a gold foil box of chocolates.

People started arriving at the appointed hour and soon the festivities were under way.

"Do I hear sixty? Remember folks, this is for The Zone," Pastor Gary said smoothly into the microphone from his perch in the gazebo.

"Eighty," called a man at the back of the crowd.

Claire strained to see over the anxious ladies standing off to the side of the gazebo. Ah, Steve Jordan was bidding on his wife's basket.

"We have eighty. Do I hear ninety?"

"I'll take that for one hundred." An older man sitting next to his striking, silver-haired wife raised his hand.

Claire's gaze swung to Steve, who was silently communicating to his wife. Claire watched the exchange as an odd yearning rose, squeezing at her chest. The couple didn't need words, just facial expressions and hand gestures Claire guessed came from years of togetherness.

She'd never experienced that kind of connectedness, that oneness only couples who truly loved each other had. She'd read about such stuff in novels and caught glimpses of it here and there, mostly between Sandy and Dave Wellington. But it was for other people, not her. Yet…

She fingered the envelope in her pocket as her gaze sought out Nick. She found him leaning casually against a tree off to the side of the festivities.

Across the crowd their eyes locked. His magnetic draw reached out to her and a maelstrom of heat flooded through her, quickening her breath and burning her cheeks.

She had felt that oneness. She'd felt that connection with Nick. She hadn't recognized it, nor understood the implications of such a phenomenon.

Deep in her heart she realized she loved him.

The thought staggered her. She clutched the back of the chair in front of her. She loved Nick.

But a gulf existed between them.

She didn't understand what drove him, what inspired such rage to fill his eyes when he looked at Tyler. She didn't know what haunted him and brought that desolate expression to his face when he didn't realize she was watching.

She wanted to shrug off her feelings. To smash the love down with the indifference and detachment that had served her so well over the years. But the feeling expanding in her chest had a life of its own and wouldn't be denied.

Walls imprison as well as protect, Nick had said.

There was truth to that. She'd tried to stay emotionally safe, had tried to keep her feelings under wraps for many years, and still ended up with the pain of loneliness. She just hadn't recognized the pain.

Until Nick roared into her life.

Still, she forced her gaze away from Nick as she tried to deal with this devastating revelation.

"Sold to the gentlemen in the front."

Claire rounded up her thoughts and focused on the proceedings. Her breath caught somewhere between her lungs and her throat as her basket was brought to the podium.

"Let's see." Pastor Gary flipped over the card with the information on it. "This beautiful, romantic basket is donated by our own Claire Wilcox. Filled with goodies for two."

Romantic? Claire smiled wanly at the sea of faces turning her way. She hadn't thought in terms of romance but, yeah, she supposed the basket had a romantic flare.

"We'll start the bidding at twenty. Do I have twenty?"

"Claire."

She turned to find Mindy's tear-stained face peering at her from around the side of the gazebo. She hurried to her. "What's wrong? Are you hurt?"

The girl shook her head. "Tyler's gone."

Claire blinked. "Gone? What happened?"

Mindy wiped at her nose. "I told him…I want to go home."

A surge of joy, of satisfaction ran rampant through Claire. Yes! This was what she'd been gently pushing for ever since she'd met Mindy. Even though Claire hadn't been able to bond with her own mother, she was happy that Mindy would be able to. Shari Vaughn had called several times, having finally accepted the truth.

Claire wrapped her arms around the teen. "I'm so proud of you." She leaned back to look into Mindy's face. "It's going to be okay."

"But I feel bad for Tyler. He doesn't have anyone. He can't go home and I don't think my mom would let me bring him home."

Claire sighed and hugged the girl again. "We'll look for Tyler, I promise. We'll find a way to make it better for him. Okay?"

Mindy gave her a watery smile. "Okay."

Keeping an arm around Mindy, Claire led her toward the front of the gazebo. "Let's go see if anyone bought my basket."

Her basket was still on the podium. Pastor Gary pointed to the side. "The gentleman bids five hundred. Do I hear six?"

Claire's mouth dropped. Five hundred dollars for her little basket? Who on earth would do such a thing? She went on tiptoe trying to see who was bidding. All she saw was a sea of faces, some she recognized, others she didn't.

"I have six from the back. Do I hear seven?"

Claire searched the rear of the audience but she missed who'd made the bid. Her gaze tripped over Nick, where he still leaned up against the tree, his arms folded across his chest, his expression neutral.

A movement in her peripheral vision caught her attention. Bob raised his arm. Her eyes widened. She didn't know what to feel about that. Flattered, but Bob? Why would he do that? She prayed he didn't expect to share it with her. Hopefully he'd decided that The Zone was a good thing.

"Seven it is." Pastor Gary looked toward the back of the crowd. "Do we have eight?"

Claire scrutinized the crowd of people. Steve Jordan was back there but he didn't make a move. She recognized the owner of the hardware store but he didn't move.

"Eight, we have eight. How about nine?"

Claire stared at the pastor. She hadn't seen anyone make a move or say anything. Who was bidding? There was a pregnant pause then, slowly, Bob lifted his hand. Claire pushed her way through the throng of ladies so she could get a better view. Lori nudged her with an elbow and gave her a grin.

The pastor smiled and inclined his head. "We have nine from the gentleman in the front. Are we going to go for a thousand?"

Claire scanned the crowd and snagged on Nick as he flexed his wrist, holding up two fingers. Ripples of excitement washed over her skin.

"Two?" Pastor Gary questioned. "Are you bidding two thousand?"

Nick nodded. Claire gasped. No way!

"The bid is two thousand." The pastor looked to Bob. Bob shook his head. "Two thousand going once. Two thousand going twice. Sold to the gentleman in the back."

There was an excited buzz through the crowd. Claire smiled feebly at the women surrounding her; their voices seemed far away as her gaze met Nick's. He gave her a slow grin that left her breathless.

A seed of hope began to sprout, taking root through the thick layer of dashed expectations surrounding her heart.

Chapter Fourteen

Two thousand for a picnic basket? At least Bob hadn't won it.

As Claire made her way through the crowd, Nick found he couldn't work up much regret for his actions. She was lovely and generous and kind, this woman who took such pains to make a difference in the lives of those around her. His respect for her grew every day.

Claire had overcome an abusive childhood, had survived life on the streets and now strove to make a safe haven for at-risk and displaced teens.

The tide of anger that ebbed and flowed within him broke, slicing a path straight through his heart. A bitter burn simmered in his veins. Regardless of his feelings for Claire, he had to end this now before either of them got hurt. He couldn't risk having another woman ripped from his life.

His faith wouldn't survive. He wouldn't survive.

"That was very generous of you, Nick," Claire stated as she stopped in front of him.

His intentions had been less than noble. She'd realize that soon enough. "Claire, let's take a walk."

As Claire fell into step with Nick, an uneasy chill pricked her skin. She rubbed her arms. They walked away from the crowded gazebo farther into the park. The scent of cut grass rose up from the ground with each step.

She glanced at Nick. How could he afford the two thousand for her basket when she'd thought he couldn't afford a hotel?

Her mouth twisted with wry amusement. His request to stay had been a ruse to keep her from being alone and unprotected, after all.

And strangely, she didn't mind. Having him around gave her a peaceful sense of security she'd never known before. And left her breathless, because he'd never promised to stay.

His somber, almost sad demeanor confused her. She worried her bottom lip. Had something happened? Did he know that Tyler had run away again?

"It went really well today," Nick stated.

"It did," she agreed. "Better than I could have imagined. The only blip on the happy meter is Tyler taking off."

His brow flickered briefly with surprise. "That's for the best. Make sure you mention that to Bob."

Claire frowned. She just didn't get it. He knew what Tyler had endured, yet he couldn't give the boy an inch. "Why should I tell Bob?"

Nick stopped walking. He stood tall and stiff. Unreachable. He looked as if he were holding a raw emotion in check. The effort thinned his lips and hardened his jaw. His eyes were hooded, as if he were deliberately trying to keep her out of his thoughts. "It's time for me to leave, Claire."

Her stomach dropped. She'd known this was coming. She expected it, but after realizing that she loved him, she couldn't fight the choking hurt crawling up her spine and settling in her throat. It was too late to pull out her detachment shield for protection. By letting herself love him, she had set herself up for more than mere disappointment.

"Where will you go?" she forced the words past the constricting lump in her throat. Her world was spinning out of control. She'd become used to him. Used to the laughter and light he'd brought into her life.

He looked toward the blue sky. His broad shoulders moved in a shrug. "I haven't decided. It doesn't matter. Anywhere."

Anywhere away from her. Agony gripped her soul. "You could stay."

He gave a terse shake of his head. "No." He ran a hand through his hair. His fingers left grooves in their wake. "I need to find peace. I have to go."

He grazed his knuckle down her cheek. She closed her eyes against the yearning his touch evoked. "You'll be okay, Claire. You're surrounded by people who love you and who want to help. Those teens aren't a threat to you anymore. There's no need for me to be here."

"But there is," she protested. "I…" She swallowed back the trepidation that told her not to go down this road. That warned she was destined for heartbreak and disappointment.

If she didn't say something, if she just let him walk away she'd be disappointed in herself.

He'd taught her it was okay to need people. That she didn't have to fear her expectations. It was okay to feel. The good and the bad. Her heart pounded so hard against her ribs she figured that any second, one would snap. "I need you."

That was as close to a declaration as she could come.

His face softened and he closed his eyes as if in pain. "I can't," he said in a harsh, raw voice. "You can't."

When he opened his eyes, the haunted hollowness of those dark depths stabbed at her.

"I'm sorry." The resignation, the defeat in those two words uttered so low she barely heard them, slammed into her like a train.

Tears stung her eyes as he took her hand and pressed a folded piece of paper into her palm. She unfolded the paper and stared. A cashier's check. Her knees threatened to buckle as the staggering amount registered. Ten thousand dollars.

"What is this?"

"A donation. A gift. It's whatever you want it to be," he said almost desperately.

"I don't want it." *I want you.*

His expression hardened. "Do what you will with it."

With long, purposeful strides he left her standing in the middle of the park holding his check, while her heart bled.

She looked over to the gazebo where the auction must have ended, because people were milling around, talking, laughing. A faint numbness hovered around the edges of the pain gripping her insides. Her detachment shield was ready. All she had to do was pick it up and cloak herself with indifference.

She knew how to mask the pain.

She started walking, slowly at first, then quicker as determination overtook the hurt.

No way was she going to let Nick off that easy. He couldn't roar into her life, turn it upside down and make her love him, and then think he could just roar out again without explaining why. Her business with Nick Andrews was not finished.

If she had her way, it was only beginning.

The Zone was quiet and still as Nick gathered his things together. He wondered where Tyler had taken off to. Would he go back to the warehouse or leave the town altogether? And how was Mindy taking Tyler's absence?

He jammed his clothes into his bag.

They are not my concern.

Yet…he should swing through nearby Beaverton to see Johnny, at least. The kid's father had up and disappeared without saying goodbye.

But I'm not the kid's father. I'm nothing to him and he's nothing to me.

Nick could use Tyler's disappearance as another excuse to stay. He could use the excuse that Claire needed him to protect her. But those excuses had lost their power. If he stayed it would be because of

Claire. If he stayed he'd be opening himself up to the risk of losing her.

He heard light footsteps coming up the stairs. Claire.

He wiped a hand over his face, trying unsuccessfully to wipe away the memory of the hurt and disappointment in her clear moist eyes.

I need you.

The words echoed in his heart, kindling to his already burning anger. He didn't want her to need him. He didn't want to need her.

He didn't want to love her.

"Seems like we've done this routine before." Claire's voice held a hard edge.

He braced himself as he turned to face her. She was leaning in the doorway with her arms folded across her chest. Her eyes bright and narrowed with determination.

"Yes, well. There won't be a repeat performance."

"No, I don't suppose there will be. But don't you think it's time to fess up and tell me what's eating away at you? I know it's more than just not wanting to go into your father's business. You can barely contain your rage when you're around Tyler. What is it with you and him? If for no other reason, appease my curiosity."

More than curiosity motivated her to press. She wanted to help, heal him. She didn't have that power. No one did.

But she did deserve the truth. He steeled himself against the wave of grief rising up to cut off his air supply. "A teenager, a runaway, killed my wife."

She made a shocked little gasp. "Oh, Nick. I'm so sorry."

She reached out to him. He jerked back.

Hugging herself, she asked in a soft voice, "What happened?"

He tightened his jaw, not wanting to say the words, to dredge up the nightmare his life had become. "I was working late one night." His lips twisted wryly. "Later than usual. I can only guess Serena needed something from the store."

He fisted his hands, feeling the consuming rage fill his soul. "I'd told her a million times it wasn't safe to be out too late at night by herself, but she was so confident that she'd be okay. She was headstrong and stubborn."

His throat contracted, he had to work to keep going. "She was in front of the store when two rival teens started fighting. One pulled out a gun." He swallowed. "Witnesses say she was caught in the middle between the two when the boy opened fire, emptying the chamber."

Claire's whole posture and attitude changed, softened. Tears gathered in her eyes. Her face took on that "let me make it better look" she'd used with the kids. He averted his gaze as she came to him. He was powerless to stop her from wrapping her arms around his waist. He took a shuddering breath. Her comfort hurt. She couldn't make it better.

A moment of silence stretched. She stepped back, then she said in a voice tight with emotion, "That must have been devastating. Are you angry that she defied you?"

"No," he said vehemently. "It wasn't her fault."

She sniffed and took a deep breath. "But you can't hold the actions of one teenager against all of them. Just because a child, a teenager, runs away doesn't automatically make them a criminal."

A bitter laugh escaped. "There you go again, protecting them."

"I'm not trying to protect anyone, Nick. I'm trying to help *you.*"

Her expression implored him to understand. He didn't. "You can't. No one can."

"Is that what you told your parents? Is that why you took off on your motorcycle, because you wouldn't let anyone help you?"

"They were smothering me with their concern. They wanted—" His fist clenched. "They want me to forgive that kid. I left because I wanted to find some peace. I just want to make sense of all this."

She moved closer and laid a warm hand on his arm. Her touch comforted, yet stirred up so much turmoil at the same time he felt a physical ache. "Sometimes life doesn't make sense. We just have to make the most out of our lives."

"How can I make the most of my life when I'm being punished for wanting a good life? I'd worked so hard to make a successful career, a stable future for us. It was all for nothing."

Her grip tightened. "You aren't being punished. God doesn't work that way."

The conviction in her voice echoed through the tiny room.

He let out a sharp breath. He'd heard that enough

after Serena's death. His parents, his pastor, his friends.

No. It had to have been his greed, his grasping for more that brought on God's wrath.

Her determined gaze tore through him. "My aunt once told me that in times of tragedy and hardship, we face the temptation to make God our adversary instead of our advocate. God's not trying to hurt you.

"And yes, He has punished people who were acting in deliberate disobedience, but that's not you. The fact that you still seek Him in the middle of your pain is a testament to your faith."

A sharp stab of misery pierced his soul. "But I can't find Him."

Her hand reached up to touch his cheek, the gesture tender and heartbreaking. "He's here, Nick. Waiting, under all the anger and hatred. He's waiting for you to rest in His love."

Nick zipped his bag and her hand fell away. The ache continued as her words bounced around his head. His heart.

She held out an envelope to him.

"This came in this morning's mail for you," she said.

He stared at the rectangular paper with narrowed eyes. Slowly he reached for it. "This is from my parents. How…?"

"I mailed your letter."

He frowned as the air left his lungs. "I'd thought I lost it."

"I found it. Mailed it."

Remembering what he'd written to them made his muscles tense and his gut tighten more. He'd told them about Claire, about the fire and the teenagers. He'd confessed his growing feelings for Claire.

He ripped open the envelope and pulled out a sheet of paper. Another folded envelope fell out and landed at his feet.

He read his mother's flowing script. A viselike pressure built in his chest. He shifted his gaze away from his mother's words to the envelope on the floor.

When would his punishment end?

Claire watched the color drain from Nick's face. His hand trembled and released the letter. It fluttered to the floor, landing so that it covered the second envelope.

Concern arced through her, battering her already wounded soul. "What is it?"

He shook his head, his features harsh, his eyes grim.

She took a hold of his hand. He felt cold to her touch. "Nick?"

He jerked away from her. His eyes glittered with fierceness. "You can't fix me. I'm not one of your projects."

She drew back. Was that how he saw her work with the teens, as a project? Her rational side said he was lashing out, directing his anger at her because she was handy. She tried for a gentle tone. "Let me help you."

His laugh was dry, brittle. "So you can feel good? Sorry, but I can't accommodate you." He kicked at the letter. "Or them."

He pushed past her and through the door.

Stung, she stood rooted to the spot as the echo of his steps slowly faded with the slam of the front door.

She picked up the letter and unopened envelope. Tears rolled down her cheeks as she read the letter, the plea from his mother for him to return, to please read the enclosed letter from the teenager who'd killed Serena—his wife.

The rumble of Nick's bike rattled Claire's composure. He was right. She couldn't help because he alone held the power to choose forgiveness.

With a sob, she ran down the stairs and out the door. She planted herself in front of his bike in the gravel driveway.

"Get out of the way, Claire."

She moved to his side where she leaned close so her words would be clearly heard. "Walls imprison as well as protect. You'll never find peace as long as you're shackled by unforgiveness. You'll never be free to live again. To love again."

She shoved the unopened envelope into his chest and kept pushing until his hand reached up to clasp her wrist.

He pulled her nearer until his mouth was close to her ear. His warm breath fanned over her cheek, drying her tears. "You're wrong."

She turned her head and pressed her lips to his and put all the love and care and hope she had within her into the kiss.

Abruptly, she broke away.

His confusion showed in his eyes. Her heart beat

furiously. She wanted to continue to lecture, to teach him and guide him to forgiveness. But deep down she knew she was done. It was all up to him now.

His choice.

She turned and walked away, feeling as if her heart was caving in on itself within the walls of her rib cage. When he revved the Harley's engine and she heard the tires crunching on the gravel as he drove out of her life, she sank to the stairs of The Zone.

"Lord, he's in your hands now. I pray you'll help him because I couldn't."

Chapter Fifteen

Claire was wrong.

As the miles zipped by on Interstate Five South, another little fissure of air blew through Nick's confidence. The first crack had opened up when she'd turned her head and kissed him.

More fissures burst through the protective layer he'd erected around his heart until the holes bled into each other, creating a gaping abyss. As he left the Portland area behind, his unease grew. Grief and oppressive condemnation settled heavy on his shoulders, making the muscles tighten and contract.

He tried to shake it. Tried to shake off the echo of Claire's words. He rolled his shoulders and the envelope sticking out of the inside pocket on his jacket stabbed at him. He jerked.

The bike wobbled, making his stomach lurch. He merged into the slow lane of the freeway and then took the next off-ramp to the frontage road. He found a gravel turnout in the brush, a place that looked to be a cop spot.

Maneuvering the bike as far out of the way as possible, he shut off the engine and removed his helmet. Something wasn't right.

Riding always took the edge off his grief. He always felt the anticipation that up ahead he'd find peace, like some sort of burger joint with a drive-up window where he could just order some calm, some sanity, as an antidote for the chaos and slicing pain of losing Serena.

But that was before Claire.

Sometimes life doesn't make sense. You have to make the most of your life.

"What life?"

He'd had a good life once. An enviable life. A wonderful marriage, a satisfying job and lots of friends. A sharp ache of loss tightened his throat.

He yanked out the envelope. "Gone. All because of this kid."

Hatred breathed fire into his soul, but quick on its tail was Claire's soft, imploring voice taking him back to that day when they'd found the three teenagers.

They're going to learn to be harder and meaner and come out angrier.

Her words were like a knife gutting his midsection, laying open his fears, his pain. Would Serena be dead if someone had tried to help the kid who had killed her? Now that boy was in jail learning to be harder, meaner. Nick had never thought about the boy beyond his own hatred. Never wondered what drove the teen to use a gun that day.

Nick hadn't cared.

Until now.

The envelope burned in his trembling hand. He slipped a finger under the seal and ripped it open. The sound of tearing paper mingled with the raggedness of his breathing.

Feeling like he was on the pinnacle of some high cliff, he withdrew the folded letter.

He didn't want to do this. Didn't want to have this kid become more than just an object of his rage. But he couldn't stop the masochistic need to read the letter. He flipped open the page. Large, scrawling words in an uneven cadence filled the lines.

Nick read the letter once quickly. His throat closed against the boulder-size knot forming in his chest. He read back through the lines, his gaze stumbling over the three words that brought a burn to the back of his eyelids.

"Please, forgive me."

He mentally scrambled away from the edge of the cliff. He crumbled the letter in his hand and threw it into the bushes. "Never!"

Then as if she were standing right next to his bike, he heard Claire's words ringing in his head. *You'll never find peace as long as you're shackled by unforgiveness.*

He started the engine with jerky movements and in a spray of gravel, pulled out onto the road.

He'd had everything he could want.

You'll never be free to live again. To love again.

Serena, dear sweet Serena. She didn't deserve to die.

"Was I too greedy, too materialistic, Lord?"

You aren't being punished. God doesn't work that way.

"If I'm not being punished Lord, then why? Why did You let this happen?"

Sometimes life doesn't make sense.

He pulled over onto the shoulder of the road again and sat, his bike idling. The breathless, teetering-on-the-edge-of-a-long-fall feeling came over him, urging him to search his heart.

The last few weeks played themselves over in his head. Claire. Brave, determined, walled-up Claire.

So full of life, so compassionate.

So afraid to be hurt.

I need you.

Nick closed his eyes as he tumbled off that cliff. For two years he'd held on to his hate and anger to keep from feeling, to keep from hurting.

And one cute blond lady with the courage of King David shamed him for his lack of faith, his lack of mercy.

One beautiful woman with the wisdom of King Saul demonstrated God's love in a tangible way.

With one former runaway he had found peace.

He opened his eyes and resolve settled in. He checked the traffic and made a U-turn. Found the gravel turnout again. It took a few moments to find the letter in the bushes. When he did, he spread it out, smoothing the wrinkles, before carefully folding it and tucking it into his pocket.

Knowing he had to make things right with his parents, he was back on the freeway headed east. He could only hold a prayer in his heart that Claire would give him another chance to claim her love when he returned.

Claire stood outside of The Zone and watched Mindy run into the arms of her mother. Shari Vaughn was a petite brunette with big eyes and a sweet smile.

Rough roads lay ahead, but the case agent who had been assigned to Mindy had assured Claire that Shari had indeed gotten rid of the abusive boyfriend. The man would be brought up on charges and Mindy would have to testify against him.

Shari was going to make a fresh start for her and her daughter in Yakima, Washington, where Shari's parents lived. Mindy was excited and nervous, but Claire knew it was for the best.

Mindy dragged her mother forward. "Mom, this is Claire."

"Hello." Claire extended her hand.

"Thank you, again," Shari said as they shook hands.

"My pleasure." Claire put an arm around Mindy, giving her a squeeze. "When you get settled, drop me a line, okay? Let me know you're all right."

Mindy turned into Claire's embrace and gave her a fierce hug. "I'll miss you."

Claire fought the tears gathering at the corners of her eyes. "I'll miss you, too. But I'll always be here if you need me."

Mindy stepped away and wiped her nose on the sleeve of the gray hooded sweatjacket. "You'll help Tyler?"

Claire nodded, not sure how she was going to manage that when he'd disappeared from town.

"Bye," Mindy said as she linked arms with her mother and walked to the blue four-door sedan Shari had arrived in.

Claire waved as the car pulled away. She heaved a contented sigh as she walked back inside. "Another successful ending. Lord, keep watch over her."

Inside The Zone an eerie silence wrapped around her, making the dull ache in her chest more acute. She found Little Nick curled up in his crate. She lifted him to her chest and hugged him close.

She missed Nick.

It'd been a week since he'd rolled out of her life, taking her heart with him. It was just her luck that when she'd come to terms with needing someone, he'd up and leave.

Over the course of the next month, amid the plans for The Zone's official opening, which had to be pushed back from July to mid-August, Claire finally located Tyler. The teen had made his way to neighboring Troutdale.

Per Bob's instructions, she went first to the police station where an Officer Nyguen had given her directions to a park where Tyler had last been seen. Once she found him, she was going to drag him back with her. The boy was self-destructive and in need of some guidance.

She found the wooded park easily. Since it was summer, the park was filled with kids and parents. A large wooden play structure dominated one end of the park with swings, monkey bars and a wobbly bridge.

Claire got out of her car and scanned the area. Her gaze snagged on a group of kids beneath a large oak tree at the far end of the grassy field. She couldn't be sure, but she thought the tall kid with his back to her was Tyler.

Mindful of the children, she worked her way around the play area. She crossed the grassy field, ducking a Frisbee, and jumping out of the way of a running black Labrador.

As she advanced on the group of boys, they fell into silence. Tyler spun around. "Wh…what are you doing here?"

Leveling a pointed stare at him, she said, "I could ask you that same question."

"Wow, man. This your mother?" a tall freckled kid with splotches of acne, asked.

An older, tougher-looking boy whistled through his teeth. "Hot. Definitely, hot."

Claire ignored them, but was amused to see Tyler shoot the rude offender a glare. She grabbed him by the hand and pulled him with her away from the influence of the boys. He jerked out of her grasp, but continued walking with her. Oh, he challenged her patience.

She gazed at him sternly. "Why'd you leave?"

His thin shoulders moved in a careless shrug beneath the red T-shirt he wore. He needed a bath and some food. Her heart twisted.

"A goodbye at least would have been nice," she said, keeping her tone even.

"Didn't think it mattered."

Claire knew that feeling, intimately. She put her hand on his arm, stopping him. "Tyler, you matter."

He scuffed his foot in the dirt and wouldn't meet her gaze.

"I want you to come back with me."

He looked up, his chin jutted out, his expression stubborn. "No."

She frowned. He was going to make her work for it. She was a trained counselor and all the methods and arguments forming in her head weren't worth the price of a warm blanket in the dead of winter if the boy didn't want to change.

I'm not one of your projects.

At the time she'd thought Nick was lashing out at her, but now she realized, his words were a truth she'd ignored.

Let them make their choice, Nick had once said.

Free will, the Bible called it.

She stared at Tyler, seeing beyond the attitude to the pain he so desperately tried to hide. He so reminded her of Gwen. The way she'd been at first.

Claire couldn't make Tyler seek help any more than she could make Nick choose to forgive. It had to come from within them.

Both Tyler and Nick needed to want to change their lives and be willing to do what was necessary. No matter how difficult.

"The Zone's open and waiting for you, Tyler. Anytime. There's no shame in asking for help."

She walked away. All she could do now was pray, and rest in God's love.

* * *

August fifteenth arrived with excitement and fanfare. The whole town, it seemed, came out for the official dedication of The Zone.

Claire bit at her lip as her gaze scanned the crowd. A bittersweet longing for Nick engulfed her. He should be here to help celebrate. He'd done so much to help make this a reality. But more than anything, she longed for his steady presence. She felt so alone and lonely. She missed Nick's companionship. She missed confiding in him. And she missed hearing his booted steps echoing through The Zone.

Every time she heard the low rumble of a motorcycle, no matter how distant, she held her breath, hoping Nick would roar back into her life.

She'd finally figured out the discrepancy between her check register and her bank balance. She'd found the checks she'd given to Nick for his weekly wages neatly stacked in one of the dresser drawers in his room. He'd given her so much, but not the one thing she really wanted. His heart.

Today, she decided, she'd stop hoping and start living her life without him.

She stood on the front steps of The Zone with Pastor Gary and the mayor of Pineridge. A microphone had been set up for them to say a few words. The crowd spilled off The Zone property, filling the street and part of the park.

The mayor, a dark-haired man in his late fifties with a thick mustache, looked impressive in a well-tailored suit and polished shoes. He spoke with the even, smooth tones of a politician. "The Zone is a needed asset to our community. The youth of Pine-ridge will find a safe and friendly environment when they venture in. The town council and I would like to thank Claire Wilcox for her willing and compassionate heart."

Applause rose, bringing heat to Claire's cheeks. The mayor handed her the microphone. Holding it tightly so her trembling hands wouldn't bob the thing against her mouth, she searched for words to express her pleasure at having her dream realized. "There are so many people who have made this a reality. I couldn't have seen this through on my own. I want to thank you all for you support, encouragement and your prayers.

"I want to dedicate The Zone to my Aunt Denise, who was my anchor when I was a teen. I..." she trailed off as her gaze landed on a tall dark-haired man who moved his way through the crowd toward her.

Nick.

Her heart tripped, skipped and stopped, only to trip and skip again. She handed the microphone to Pastor Gary and hurried down the steps. Jostling her way through the crowd, she met him in the middle amid a sea of people and curious stares.

"You're here," she breathed out in a rush.

His grin was devastating. Welcomed. Loved. She wanted to wrap her arms around him. To tell him how much she'd missed him. But she held back as old fears buzzed around like little gnats drawn to sweet fruit.

He took her hand and pulled her through the crowd until they were standing on the edge where an older couple she'd never seen before, but would recognize anywhere, stood. Nick's parents.

His father stood as tall as Nick and had the same dark, watchful eyes, and the same hard line to his jaw. His mother was arresting, with jet-black hair swept up in a fancy twist and warm brown eyes that regarded her with interest.

"Mom, Dad. This is Claire. Claire, Victor and Olivia Andrews."

In a bit of a daze, Claire shook hands with Nick's parents.

"Nick has told us so much about you, I feel I already know you," Olivia stated warmly in that east coast accent that Claire had come to love in Nick.

"Thank you for everything," Victor Andrews said with meaning.

She barely heard him. All she could think, all she could see was Nick. "You went home."

The warmth of his smile echoed in his voice. "I did."

Awed and pleased, she could only smile wider. If he went home then...

She blinked. Then what?

"Why are you here?" Her breath stalled in her lungs with possibilities. Was he back to stay? Just to visit? Could she dare hope he'd come for her?

He captured her hand, his grip sure and strong. "Mom, Dad. Excuse us."

"Of course, Son."

His father's knowing tone confused Claire. All of this confused her. "Where—"

"I'll answer all your questions. I promise."

She allowed Nick to lead her farther away from the throng of people to a quiet spot behind a flowering rhododendron.

"I came back, Claire, because I don't like being shackled. I want to live again."

Her mouth went dry. She swallowed. She had to ask because she had nothing to lose. She had no expectations. Only hope. "Are you free to live again?"

"Yes. I went to see that kid." His dark gaze held compassion. "You were right, Claire. If someone had reached out to that kid…"

Tears gathered at the corner of her eyes. "And what about love?"

He reached up to caress her cheek. His tender expression captivated her. "I found love, right here, Claire."

Her breath hitched. "You did?"

He nodded. "I love you, Claire."

Her heart beat so fast and hard she thought it might burst from her chest. Only hope. Only love. A wave of joy washed through her. There were no doubts, no hesitation. "I love you."

"Good." And his lips descended onto hers, warm and tender. She lost herself in the melding of their breaths, the sweetness of love.

"You're going have to marry her if you keep that up."

They jerked apart. Claire gaped at the kid standing a few feet away. Tyler. Same jutting chin, same challenging gaze, same attitude.

She held her breath as she turned her gaze back to Nick, dreading to see the hatred and rage. But his eyes crinkled at the corners with amusement. Her heart melted into a puddle at his feet. He truly was free.

"You've got that right, my friend," Nick said. His hands gently framed her face. "Claire, will you marry me?"

One question still burned on her heart. "What about The Zone?"

The corners of his mouth rose. "I thought we made a good team."

She blinked back her tears of joy. "We did."

His thumb rubbed across her bottom lip. "We do," he corrected. "You still haven't answered my question."

Full-fledged happiness exploded within her and the tears fell in earnest. "Yes. Oh, yes."

Her heart sang a song of praise as she slipped into the shelter of Nick's loving embrace.

Thank You, God, for answered prayers.

Epilogue

Twenty-month-old Rebecca Andrews lifted her chubby finger toward the end of the room. Her yellow sundress rode high and showed off her ruffled diaper cover. "Mommy, yook! Dare Tiyer!"

"Yes, sweetie. There's Tyler," Claire whispered to the raven-haired toddler squirming in her father's lap.

On the stage at the front of the auditorium, Tyler Riggs, wearing a blue gown and matching square hat with a gold tassel, extended his right hand to the principal of Pineridge High School and reached for his diploma with his left hand. The tall teen flashed a grin at the audience as he held up the scrolled paper in a victory salute. His once scraggly hair now sported a hip style that Claire's hairdresser friend, Lori, swore was all the rage with the young hunks in Hollywood.

"What a goof," Gwen remarked with a wide grin of her own, as she clapped loudly from her seat on the other side of Claire.

Claire met her husband's gaze over the head of their daughter as they clapped with enthusiasm. The pride and love swelling in Claire's chest reflected in Nick's dark eyes.

Tyler had matured and was fast becoming the man Claire knew he could be. The man God wanted him to be. With Nick's help, Tyler had formulated a plan for his future. Two years at Mount Hood College, then off to Eugene to study architecture at the University of Oregon.

That wasn't to say the last three years had been easy. Tyler had come to live with them at The Zone and the adjustment had been tough on all of them at first, despite the love that grew daily between her and Nick.

Thankfully Sandy and Dave had become parenting mentors to Claire and Nick and had assured them that Tyler's attitude and actions were typical for his age, regardless of the scars left by his childhood.

With firm boundaries and love, they weathered the storm of building trust and respect. Claire was proud not only of Tyler, but of her husband, as well. Nick had proved himself to be an excellent father figure for Tyler.

She put her hand on her growing abdomen, her gaze going to little Rebecca. And an amazing father for their own children. Their legacy.

Every day she thanked God for the gift of Nick. With their marriage she gained a wonderful, loving husband, a child she adored, another due to arrive in four months and caring in-laws. She never imagined she could be so happy.

God had blessed The Zone, as well, with donations and support from the community. She and Nick had had the opportunity to help many teens over the last few years. She'd never forget any of them or the richness they'd brought to her life. And God willing, there would be more. She still kept in contact with Johnny and Mindy. The first two success stories of The Zone.

Johnny was headed to Portland State in the fall. And Mindy and her mom, Shari, were leaving for Florida to be near Shari's sister's family. Mindy promised to write as soon as they were settled. She hoped to get a job at Disney World while she attended the local community college in Orlando.

And then there was Gwen. Claire glanced over at the woman who'd become like a younger sister. Gwen's long red hair fell over her shoulder in her traditional braid and her bright rust-colored blouse accentuated her amber eyes. Claire was proud of her and would miss her when she left at the end of the month to start her new job as a physician's assistant in Seattle—a long way from the streetwise kid that had come to live with her and Aunt Denise.

Claire was so grateful for the blessings in her life. Her husband and children. Gwen. Tyler. The teens.

The Zone had become what she'd envisioned. A safe haven for kids in need. A place for them to go to when running away seemed like the only option. She was making a difference.

She leaned over and kissed the top of Rebecca's head.

"How about me?" Nick asked, his eyes filled with

tenderness. The collar of his royal blue polo shirt was bunched up in Rebecca's fist. His strong hands held their daughter with the utmost gentleness, steadying her as she stood with one sandal-clad foot on each of his khaki-covered thighs.

Deep abiding love filled Claire's heart and brought tears to her eyes. Nick had made a difference in her life. One that could have only come from God. "Always."

Their lips met and Claire sighed with contentment.

* * * * *

Dear Reader,

Thank you for reading my second novel with Steeple Hill Love Inspired. I hope you enjoyed Claire and Nick's journey as they overcame the pain of the past to discover *A Sheltering Love*.

As I did the research for this story, I was touched by the plight of homeless teens. The many stories I read brought me to tears. And I discovered homelessness among the youth in this country is reaching crisis proportions in every city in every state. Young people are routinely sleeping in parks, abandoned buildings, alleys and doorways. Lacking guidance, many turn to drugs, crime and violence. Without intervention the street culture becomes home and family.

But there are many, like Claire, who've stepped up to the plate and are trying to make a difference by supporting their local teen shelters.

May God bless you always,

And now, turn the page
for a sneak preview of
UNDER COVER OF DARKNESS
by Elizabeth White
Part of Steeple Hill's exciting new series,
Love Inspired Suspense!
On sale in July 2005
from Steeple Hill Books.

Prologue

Eagle Pass, Texas

The black iron skeleton of the old railroad bridge known as *el puente negro* arched across the Rio Grande in bold relief against a clear, starlit sky. The odors of jasmine, fish and mud drifted on a damp summer breeze down to the two uniformed men searching the riverbank.

U.S. Border Patrol agent Jack Torres struggled through tall banks of carrizo cane as he followed behind his partner, their powerful flashlights cutting a path through the heavy vegetation. They were looking for broken stalks that would indicate human movement, listening for the sounds of fearful panting and rustling, the telltale ripple of water.

Jack stopped Rico by touching his elbow. "Too quiet around here, man," he whispered. "Something's wrong."

"I know," Rico agreed. "Not even a bullfrog singin' us a lullaby."

Shoulders tight, Jack moved closer to the water. The illegals often chose to come across under the bridge, where the darkness hid them until they crawled right up into the cane along the bank. Jack wondered how they could stand it. He had recurring nightmares about going under, sucking river water into his lungs. Submersion had always scared him; he'd had to make himself learn to swim just before going into the Academy.

They stood listening until Rico, always hyper, started to move. Jack motioned for him to wait. "Turn off your light."

Rico complied. "We should've been off thirty minutes ago," he grumbled under his breath. "Isabel worries when I don't call."

"I'll tell her you were unavoidably detained."

Jack lifted his night-vision glasses to scan the blackness downriver. Not so long ago the only thing ground agents worried about was controlling the swimmers. They came across without benefit of steel or pavement—some on rafts or inner tubes, many floating on planks or doors, most simply dog-paddling across. Lately, however, as dope peddlers moved into Piedras Negras over in Mexico, the action had gotten a little more interesting.

"Did you hear about Zuniga and Berg?" Rico said.

Jack loved Rico like a brother, but he wished he'd shut up. Had that been a footfall on the bridge? He couldn't be sure. He trained the glasses on the apex, but didn't see anything.

Rico kept whispering. "Last week they caught three MAK-90s. Sixty-one-hundred rounds of ammo, too. Then the very next night they picked up 450 pounds of marijuana. Can you believe that, man?"

Rico talked too much when he was nervous. Jack knew his partner was tired, had been up till all hours last night with a sick kid. Maybe they should call it quits after all—

The noise on the bridge again. Louder, footsteps running, a body slamming against the side rail, somebody yelling Spanish curses. Where were the border patrol guys at the checkpoint?

The lights on the bridge went out.

Jack stood up, heart pounding, hand on his gun. *"¡Párese y identífiquese!"* he shouted. "Rico, cover me." The running continued. *"¡Dije, 'Párese!'"* Jack stumbled toward the bridge, finally clear of the cane, but briars and other weeds caught at his clothes.

A gun fired, the bullet whizzed past his shoulder. Jack dove into the cane for cover. More gunfire blasted—deafening, confusing, bursting in obscene pops, making it impossible to identify the direction of the sound.

"Oh, God, protect us!" Jack groaned. "Rico, where are you?" He didn't know if his partner could hear him or not through the noise.

Where was Rico? He looked around, afraid to shoot because he couldn't find him. *Oh, God let him be all right.*

Shots blasted overhead again, and this time Jack placed the sound at the base of the bridge, only a hundred yards away. He raised up, saw three dark shapes running toward him; he fired and saw one of the figures fall. The other two split, one plunging into the river, the other disappearing.

As suddenly as the fusillade had begun, it was over. Numb dark silence dropped into place. Where was his backup? The agents from the bridge should have come running at the first sound of gunfire.

"Lord my God, please don't let any of those guys be down." Jack got up on his hands and knees. He looked around and heard nothing, then half stood, chest heaving. The gun shook in his hand as if it were alive. He staggered to his feet.

"Rico?" he whispered into the unnatural stillness. Cold hard stars blinked in the sky. Rico was worse than a kid, playing tricks. "Rico, I'm telling you this isn't funny. I nearly got my shoulder blown off."

He stepped backward, turned around.

"Rico!" he shouted. Then he moved to the edge of the water, where the cane was crushed in a zigag path.

The lights on the bridge flickered back on, and the wail of a siren blared from the direction of the city.

Jack remembered his flashlight. He turned it on and, slipping, nearly falling, shone it into the broken cane.

Broken cane. Broken cane. Water. Red water. Blood.

Rico.

SECOND CHANCE MOM

BY

MARY KATE HOLDER

Jared Campbell needed a wife to keep his late sister's
adopted children together. Annie Dawson seemed
the perfect choice for the Australian farmer. Until
Jared learned Annie's shocking secret: the youngest
boy was her son. Was Annie's second chance to be
a mom going to be ruined because of Jared's
"issues" with adoption...or could his wounded
heart find healing with his new family?

Don't miss SECOND CHANCE MOM
On sale June 2005

Available at your favorite retail outlet.

LOVING FEELINGS

BY

GAIL GAYMER MARTIN

Calling the police on an eight-year-old wasn't
something Todd Bronski was willing to do…
especially not after he met Jenni Anderson. As
Cory's guardian, she was trying to do the best
for her nephew. Becoming her business partner
meant Todd would spend even more time with the
boy—and his lovely aunt. But Jenni wasn't sure
she was ready to mix business with romance….

Don't miss LOVING FEELINGS
On sale June 2005

Available at your favorite retail outlet.

Take 2 inspirational love stories FREE!

PLUS get a FREE surprise gift!

Mail to Steeple Hill Reader Service™

In U.S.
3010 Walden Ave.
P.O. Box 1867
Buffalo, NY 14240-1867

In Canada
P.O. Box 609
Fort Erie, Ontario
L2A 5X3

YES! Please send me 2 free Love Inspired® novels and my free surprise gift. After receiving them, if I don't wish to receive anymore, I can return the shipping statement marked cancel. If I don't cancel, I will receive 4 brand-new novels every month, before they're available in stores! Bill me at the low price of $4.24 each in the U.S. and $4.74 each in Canada, plus 25¢ shipping and handling and applicable sales tax, if any*. That's the complete price and a savings of over 10% off the cover prices—quite a bargain! I understand that accepting the books and gift places me under no obligation ever to buy any books. I can always return a shipment and cancel at any time. Even if I never buy another book from Steeple Hill, the 2 free books and the surprise gift are mine to keep forever.

113 IDN DZ9M
313 IDN DZ9N

Name	(PLEASE PRINT)	
Address	Apt. No.	
City	State/Prov.	Zip/Postal Code

Not valid to current Love Inspired® subscribers.

Want to try two free books from another series?
Call 1-800-873-8635 or visit www.morefreebooks.com.